Cool fingers cupped his cheeks. Shelby looked earnestly into his eyes. She pulled his face closer. Conor didn't resist.

She kissed him.

Nothing like that peck on the cheek yesterday—this was a kiss. A real kiss. Soft lips, warm breath and all. The kind that made a guy dream. And he let the sensation roll through him, because it had been a long time since a woman's kiss had felt like this. Like Shelby.

A red flag waved frantically in his mind as her mouth continued to wreak havoc with his. She gave 100 percent of herself, as she always did, and he reciprocated, holding her closer, pressing his mouth harder, until he felt a familiar thrill down to his toes. Friends would've stopped long before now. Who did she think she was kidding, pretending they could revert back, when this was anything *but* the kiss of a *friend*?

* * *

THE DELANEYS OF SANDPIPER BEACH:
A family business with room to grow...

Dear Reader,

Where would we be without second chances in life? We're far too human to always get things right the first time around. Sometimes we need a few more years under our belts before we wise up and see what we've missed. Other times, someone else makes a decision that we have no control over, and we suffer the consequences. The most important thing is to seize that opportunity to get it right when it comes around again.

Fortunately, in *Reunited with the Sheriff*, Conor Delaney and Shelby Lynn Brookes get that second chance. Both may be older and wiser, but are they also willing to admit their mistakes? As always, when two people remember the same situation—in this case a lifetime of friendship that turned to love early on, and continued with a special promise—they both have their own take. Where Conor thought he was being supportive of Shelby's dream to become a chef, Shelby felt he was pushing her away. When Shelby wants to start over, Conor doesn't think it's possible to erase the past.

That leaves the big question: Will these two meant-to-be lovebirds get over their issues to give their romance another try? Stick around for some surprises, fireworks and that guaranteed happily-ever-after, Conor and Shelby style.

Thanks for reading,

Lynne

www.LynneMarshall.com

Reunited with the Sheriff

Lynne Marshall

Recycling programs
for this product may
not exist in your area.

ISBN-13: 978-1-335-46577-1

Reunited with the Sheriff

Printed in U.S.A.

Lynne Marshall used to worry she had a serious problem with daydreaming, and then she discovered she was supposed to write those stories down! A late bloomer, she came to fiction writing after her children were nearly grown. Now she battles the empty nest by writing romantic stories about life, love and happy endings. She's a proud mother and grandmother who loves babies, dogs, books, music and traveling.

Books by Lynne Marshall

Harlequin Special Edition

American Heroes
Soldier, Handyman, Family Man

The Delaneys of Sandpiper Beach
Forever a Father

Her Perfect Proposal
A Doctor for Keeps
The Medic's Homecoming
Courting His Favorite Nurse

Harlequin Medical Romance

Miracle for the Neurosurgeon
A Mother for His Adopted Son
200 Harley Street: American Surgeon in London
Her Baby's Secret Father

Summer Brides
Wedding Date with the Army Doc

The Hollywood Hills Clinic
His Pregnant Sleeping Beauty

Cowboys, Doctors...Daddies!
Hot-Shot Doc, Secret Dad
Father for Her Newborn Baby

Visit the Author Profile page
at Harlequin.com for more titles.

This book is dedicated to the
loyal Special Edition readers, and
everyone who believes in second-chance love.

Prologue

Conor Delaney and Shelby Brookes strolled Sandpiper Beach at sunset while still euphoric from making love. Earlier that month, on a Fourth of July hike, they'd found an abandoned house on the cliffs with a spectacular view to watch fireworks. The Beacham House, the sign hanging lopsided from one chain link out front had said. Since that day, they'd met there just about every afternoon. Sex with a distant ocean view, well, there was nothing quite like it. On brisk evenings, like tonight, they'd even used the fireplace with the functioning chimney.

"What if we hadn't run into each other?" He brought up something that had been on his mind since that first day.

Shelby glanced up at Conor, the mischievous sparkle in her eyes he'd come to live for, her long hair lifting with the breeze and riling up his insides all over again. "It's an awfully small town, I think we were bound to."

Without a doubt, he believed her. But even once they

reunited, with him staying at The Drumcliffe Hotel under the ever-vigilant eyes of his grandfather, mother and father, and Shelby's mother just back from a two-week Canadian Rockies trip, they'd needed a place to meet—alone. Then they took that hike and, well, the Fourth of July fireworks took on a whole new meaning. He tugged her closer to his side as she snuggled in, their steps in near-perfect unison thanks to him measuring his strides.

"Do you think it was meant to be?" she continued.

Now she'd started to sound like his grandfather, the man who thought everything happened for a reason. Like finding that house. But there was some merit to what she'd implied. Four years since they'd last seen each other after high school graduation, they'd both come home unplanned to Sandpiper Beach at the same time. He'd recently graduated with a criminal justice degree and had already completed the basic training for peace officers in California at the Police Academy. He'd come home to wait out the summer for results from background checks from the sheriff departments he'd applied to in three nearby counties. She'd come home because she'd lost her job, without further prospects back east.

"I did give you a promise ring before you left." He'd carefully chosen a Claddagh ring when he'd found out her plans to go to culinary school in NYC. She was the first girl he'd fallen in love with way back in tenth grade. Maybe even since fourth grade, when they met playing tetherball.

"You haven't exactly been courting me since then, though."

True, they'd fallen far out of touch in four years.

"That's a little hard when you're in New York and I'm in California." It was a defensive and lame response, because he also wondered why he hadn't tried harder with her, kept in touch, let her know he still thought about her. Often.

"In fact, you're the one who sent me away!"

Yes, he'd encouraged her to go, trying to be wise about waiting until they were older, and never wanting to give Shelby a reason to resent him for holding her back. That was the distinct sense he'd secretly held about his mother with his father, and her painting. His parents had gotten married right out of high school, then had a kid, and she never had the chance to study her craft. Her passion. Unlike his father, he'd never want to do that to someone he loved.

"You wanted to go, it was your dream."

"I know, but still." Was it hurt he saw in her questioning eyes?

After high school, Shelby had gone east and he'd begun his studies in San Diego. They both needed to find their way in the world before they could commit to more. Ever Mr. Practical, that was what he'd told himself back then. *Do the right thing. Wait until you have something to offer her.* "I didn't want to be the reason you couldn't go after what you wanted."

She looked down, kicked some sand with her toes. "We both had dreams."

"And look what we've achieved at twenty-three? Maybe running into each other was our reward."

"That's what I'm saying," she said. "What are the odds that we'd both wind up home at the same time?"

They stopped for the moment, gazing into each other's eyes. *Their meeting up out of the blue was extraordinary when he thought about it.* Or had Grandda planted a little thought in his head about "the word" being a certain someone was coming home? Padraig, Sandpiper's own gadabout, always kept his hands on the pulse of their hometown.

For whatever reason, they'd found paradise at their secret hideaway for nearly four weeks. Like nothing he'd ever experienced with a woman before. As far as he was concerned, she was "the one" and he was so glad to find her again. The only way he knew how to show how he felt was to kiss her again, so he did.

Shelby welcomed Conor's kiss.

They'd spent every day together for the past month, and everything had been wonderful.

After graduating high school, instead of going to college, Shelby had enrolled in culinary school and headed off to lower Manhattan. Completing the course in two years, she held a series of so-so jobs before getting her first challenge at one of NYC's trendy new restaurants, but the business had gone under in less than two years. She wasn't proud of giving up and coming home, so she called it "taking a breather."

Finding Conor again, her first love and most trusted friend, had been nothing short of amazing. Especially after enduring the loneliness from being in NYC for so long, chasing her dreams, getting knocked down, refusing to give up. They'd picked right up like they'd never been apart. Friends. Lovers. Now it was their last night, and Conor's kiss tasted bittersweet.

"This was a perfect summer," he said, breaking away from her lips.

Though smiling demurely, she was totally aware of how much she'd opened his world. They'd both obviously been with other people, learned more about making love since their early, sometimes awkward times together. He'd delivered her first hickey in middle school. Later, in high school, they'd been virgins together. Though their natural chemistry had always been strong, something explosive had happened between them this summer. A quick flash of what they'd been doing a few short minutes earlier made her need to kiss him again.

Perfect summer, yes. But nothing stayed perfect for long. Just yesterday she'd gotten word that a forgotten job application as a sous-chef in an established and respected restaurant in New York City, had finally opened up. The job was hers for the taking, but she had to leave ASAP. Just when things were really heating up with Conor. The problem was, when she'd first applied for that job and several others, so desperate to work and prove herself as a chef, she would have given anything for the position. Now Conor, without trying, interfered with that perspective. Was she still bound and determined to prove herself? Or could a sexy distraction like Conor change her mind?

She couldn't let all the training and work she'd put in for the past four years go to waste. It was still her dream, on her terms. But did he have to be so understanding about it?

It was bad timing. And definitely not part of their "meant to be" summer. Still, Conor refused to stand in the way. He'd used some corny explanation, "The Grandda" view, he'd called it. In other words, this, too, was probably meant to offer them more time to grow. After all, they were only a few years out of high school and he was just starting out on his law enforcement career. But one day they'd be ready and nothing would stop them, even if she had to beg him to move back east.

Thinking while kissing was never a good idea. Doubt tumbled over her: Why was he always so supportive of her leaving to pursue her dreams? Especially now, after their beautiful summer? Would he move if she asked him? Insecurity, like a tight net, held her stiff and still.

And Conor had noticed.

* * *

Midkiss, with the tumbling ocean as the backdrop, a crazy idea flew into Conor's mind. He ended the kiss, sensing she'd tensed up.

"This was the best summer of my life," Conor said, cupping Shelby's face, confident about love, true love, and overlooking her questioning gaze. "Let's make a promise."

Normally practical-minded to a fault, tonight anything but, he'd stopped her under the second lifeguard station from The Drumcliffe Hotel. At dusk, with the low tide tickling the shore, the brisk summer breeze seeming to encircle them in their own world, Conor held Shelby's shoulders, brushing her lips with his, working up the confidence to suggest more.

Letting Shelby go after he'd found her again was the last thing he wanted to do, but he couldn't keep her from her dream to run her own top-notch kitchen. In her mind, New York was the best and only place in the States to get experience. Yet he couldn't let her go without a promise, a real promise this time, not some corny Claddagh ring.

How long was he willing to wait for Shelby to build her career? How long could they be true to each other long distance? Only the test of time would tell…with the help of a promise.

"A promise?" Shelby's deep brown eyes gazed into his, seeming to buy into any wild plan he concocted.

"Yes, let's promise, no matter what—you do your thing, I'll do mine—but let's meet right here at sunset in four years." He pulled out his phone and checked a future calendar for the date and day and repeated it to her. "Will you promise?"

Her gaze widened, the newly rising moon reflecting in her fawn-colored irises.

"I'll have a question for you then," he said, lifting a

brow, teasing out the promise, "and we'll see." *If our love is meant to be forever.*

Her quivery smile, and the chill bumps appearing across her shoulders and chest gave him hope.

"Yes, I promise," she said on a breath, sending his spirits soaring.

"Shelby Lyn Brookes, I love you," he said.

"I love you," she repeated, dreamy-looking and beautiful as the setting sun.

They sealed their plans with the kind of kiss they'd gotten especially good at that summer. Deep, drawn-out and filled with need. And this time, heated with a promise. Then they headed back to the Beacham House for their last night together in Sandpiper Beach.

Chapter One

Six years, seven months and nearly three weeks later...

Conor Delaney pulled his used muscle car into his designated parking spot at the family hotel, revved the engine, then turned the key. He liked old stuff, like this beat-up Camaro painted mostly with primer. And the old Beacham House, empty and begging for someone to buy it and bring it to life again, sitting far back on the cliffs above the Sandpiper beach dunes. That was a whole other story. He liked The Drumcliffe, too—the vintage hotel he'd grown up in and around, just footsteps from the beach. *Thanks, Grandda, for thinking about the future way back in the 1960s and buying the land.* Though Conor wasn't exactly proud that at twenty-nine he still lived in the family hotel.

Tonight, he was especially glad he had the hotel restaurant at his fingertips. It had been a long Saturday, with several drunk and disorderly arrests at a local sports bar, no time for a lunch break, and, after the end of his shift, he was hungry. Really hungry. He thought about ordering room service so he could strip out of his deputy sheriff uniform and eat in his boxers and undershirt in front of the TV, but something nudged him to be sociable. A guy could only dodge his mother for so long before she came knocking on his hotel suite door—that was a major drawback of living at home at his age even if it was a noble cause to save money for that dream fixer-upper.

Again, another story.

Opening the car door, he stretched out his left leg, and thanks to the low-to-the-ground chassis, took his sweet time standing all the way up. They didn't make cars like this with guys six foot three in mind. He straightened his shoulders, eyes on the prize—dinner!—no worries about needing reservations on a Saturday night because, well, this was The Drumcliffe Hotel Restaurant. The chef, Rita, was like a hundred or something, and the regulars were mostly senior citizens.

Conor's brother Mark was taking over more and more responsibility with the hotel, now that Mom and Dad were on their countdown to retirement, and he had big plans, too. Or so it seemed. But since Mark had moved in with Laurel in the B&B across the street, and Conor had lost his last brother/roommate, he hadn't caught up with all of Mark's latest plans. He kind of missed their late-night catch-up talks, too. Now that he roomed with his first cousin from Ireland, Brian, the late-night conversations all centered around getting to know each other. A whole different thing.

Walking into the dark dining room, he saw more heads above the leather booths than usual, and something smelled great. Man, he was hungry.

The local high school girl playing hostess for the week-end smiled. "Hi, Mr. Delaney. Dining alone?"

He nodded.

Looking a little doe-eyed in the dim lighting, the long-haired brunette led the way to the family booth back in the far corner, then handed him the menu. Not the usual one, but a new narrow one-pager, in fuchsia. He perused the column of Today's Specials written in a fancy font, and was surprised to see Rita had changed things up. Where was the pot roast, the meat loaf, the poached salmon?

Instead, he found a list of meals he'd never seen before, including beef tenderloin steaks on potato galettes with mustard sauce. What the hell was a potato galette? Organic farm-raised chicken breasts with fresh garlic and rosemary, sweet potato mash and kale. *Who ate kale on purpose?* Pan-seared tuna? Had Rita started smoking something besides her Virginia Slims?

When Abby, the long-term waitress, arrived to take his order, he lifted his brows and held out the menu. "What's up?"

"New chef."

"Rita retired and I didn't hear about a party?"

"It's next week."

Maybe his crazy work schedule had finally caught up to him. "Okay, then." He glanced at the menu again. "Well, what do you recommend?"

"I'm hearing great things about the beef tenderloins to-night. You'll love those potatoes. Tried 'em myself earlier."

Too hungry to think about heading up the street to the Bee Bop Diner for a burger, he ordered a beer from his grandfather's adjacent pub and agreed to the beef dish. "Can a guy still get a green salad?"

"Of course, fresh baby greens—organic, of course," Abby said before listing a series of weird new dressings.

With his hungry mind thoroughly boggled he shrugged. "Just… I'll take the white wine and shallot one. Whatever." *What was going on?*

He seriously worried about the fate of his family's hotel if the restaurant went under. People in this small beach community didn't like change, and many had been coming here for decades for inexpensive, traditional meals. That was another thing he'd noticed, a price hike for dinners. Not huge, but there nevertheless. He didn't care because he didn't have to pay, but what about the locals?

While he waited for food and drink, he thumbed through his phone wondering what a shallot was. Read a few lame tweets, checked his text messages and got sidetracked with an attached article in an email. His beer came, and shortly after, his salad arrived, which tasted better than any he'd ever had from Rita. Changing up the dressings turned out to be a great idea. Or maybe the improvement had something to do with using fresh spring greens other than iceberg and romaine?

When his main course arrived, plated like nothing he'd ever seen at The Drumcliffe before—the perfectly medium rare tenderloin was sliced and balanced on an oval mound of brown and crisp sliced potatoes, and topped with mustard sauce and fresh parsley—where had they found the new chef?

Half-starved, he dug right in, deciding to leave the questions for after dinner. Wow, was his mouth happy about that decision. Several times he sat straight, purposely slowing down his chewing to savor the flavors and tenderness of the meat. And Abby was right about the potatoes. They tasted like a little piece of starch-and-butter heaven, with a hint of cheese. They were so good they had to be bad for him.

"What do you think?" His mother appeared at his

booth. She seemed to be primped up more than usual for the Saturday night crowd, her natural red hair cut just below her earlobes, parted on the side in a classic style, her green eyes sparkling like she had a big secret. Wearing beige slacks and a top nearly the same color as her eyes, Maureen Delaney slid into the booth across from him.

He shook his head, smiled with sealed lips because his cheeks were crammed full of the delicious food. He swallowed half of it. "Best meal I've ever had here. Ever had *anywhere*."

Maureen grinned, seeming to enjoy watching him eat as if she'd cooked it herself. When his plate was scraped clean, he pushed it away.

"My compliments to the chef. That was, hands down, the best meal I've ever tasted."

"Ever?" Obviously surprised, she gave a relieved smile.

"Ever. And you can tell whoever replaced Rita, I said so."

Maureen sat still, weighing her thoughts. "Why don't you tell her, yourself?"

He had thoroughly enjoyed his meal, and they'd obviously hired someone who knew what she was doing. With him being out of the loop and chronically busy with work, just like he'd missed Rita's last day, he'd probably missed the new employee newsflash, too. Who read hotel memos, when he had to read hundreds a day at work?

He understood the value of a good chef and a compliment for a new and nervous cook would probably go far, so he agreed. "Okay."

Conor finished his beer and headed for the hotel kitchen, aware his mother stayed behind at the booth. Grinning, and ready to do his good deed for the day, he barreled through the door to the busy and hectic kitchen.

"That was the best dinner I've ever had. My compliments to the chef!"

He scanned the activity and zeroed in on the area of the stove, to a petite female in a double-breasted pink chef jacket with gray cuffs and a matching slate chef beret, her short light brown hair barely sticking out from beneath. At the sight, a sudden ball of emotion wound tight and rolled from his chest to his overly stuffed stomach, then dropped to his knees, locking them, and he came to a dead stop.

Shelby. Lyn. Brookes. Turned out the new chef was the woman who'd not only broken, but ripped out, stepped on and chucked his heart into the ocean exactly two years, seven months and three weeks ago. Not that he was counting.

She looked as stunned as he was. Busy juggling various dishes at the eight-burner stove, obviously flustered, her hand slipped, spilling a bottle of something that looked like whiskey over a thick and quickly grilling steak, and onto the gas flames. A fire flashed, like a magic trick going awry, and she jumped back, her previous rattled expression turning to pure fear. She squealed as a blanket of smoke covered her, and he sprung to action.

Being in a job like his, one filled with surprises and challenges, and having grown up in and around the hotel kitchen, he wasn't dealing with his first fire. Conor had the presence of mind to locate, rip from the wall and use the extinguisher over the flaming steak and burners, putting out the fire in record time…at the expense of a prime cut of meat and a few other meats grilling nearby. At least he'd avoided the blare of a fire alarm. He kept the most unexpected and unwelcomed meeting with the new hotel chef between him and her, and, oh, the startled restaurant crew…who all stood around with mouths agape and eyes wide.

* * *

Shelby couldn't believe what'd just happened, or the fact Conor Delaney had put out the fire she'd started. Because of him!

She knew she'd have to face him at some point when she'd applied for and accepted the job offer from Mark Delaney. Her choices were nil back east and she needed to regroup before moving on. Now here she was facing down the guy she'd left behind. The guy she'd betrayed. The guy she used to love like no other.

And setting a fire.

Why did he have to come for dinner on her very first night at The Drumcliffe?

Seeing Conor, the sweetest person she'd ever known, all grown up and devastatingly good-looking in that deputy sheriff's uniform, she'd lost control of her hands. It didn't help that she was overcome with a huge surge of guilt. Good thing he'd had the sense to grab the fire extinguisher.

Conor set the empty extinguisher on the stainless-steel counter, leveled her with a haunting stare, reminding her how careless she'd been with their promise, then left without a word.

Maureen showed up. "You okay? Everyone okay?"

Shaken, Shelby gave a nod. Her sous-chef began tossing the fried meat and ruined food into the trash. The kitchen cleanup crew—one mature woman from housekeeping looking for extra shifts—took over from there.

Maureen draped her arm over Shelby's shoulders. "No burns? You sure you're okay?"

"I just need a minute. I'll make up for this." She couldn't lose her job, not on her first night. She had dinners to cook, people to feed. A reputation to save.

"I know you can," Maureen said with a sympathetic gaze.

Rather than stand there shaking, Shelby jumped back to work, and while she did, her mind worked overtime.

Slapped-down by life, and now a devout realist, she knew the only way to make her dreams of becoming a great chef come true was to start small, to prove herself, work her way up from there, then one day run her own first-rate NYC kitchen. *Not to depend on anyone but herself.* Maybe, if she worked hard enough, she could put The Drumcliffe Restaurant on the map in Central Coast California. But not if she burned the place down first!

Grabbing a fresh pan, she chose another prize cut of beef, seasoned and buttered it before placing it on the cleaned grill. "Abby?" She called over the waitress who'd ordered the steak. "Please give a complimentary appetizer to your table for the wait, but let them know their meal will be right out, okay?"

The waitress gave a smiling agreement, grabbed a large prong shrimp appetizer from the iced waiting bin and left.

Sure Shelby knew her new job almost certainly guaranteed she'd see Conor. Mark had warned her Conor still lived at the hotel when he'd hired her, and realizing it would be inevitable, she'd been prepared. But man-oh-man, she was anything but when Conor had walked into her kitchen.

Instead of quitting on the spot, she was determined to prove that after all those years in New York, she hadn't wasted her training in culinary school. She belonged in this kitchen. But seeing Conor immediately reminded her how much she used to care for him, and the fact he was a living, breathing heartthrob hadn't helped a bit. He seemed to have just kept on growing, looking larger than life. And handsome, oh, momma, was he handsome.

Here she was at twenty-nine, still trying to hit her stride, find her place in the world, and he was obviously a grown-up, dependable, responsible man in uniform. The polar opposite of all the other men in her life since leaving Sandpiper Beach.

She flipped the steak, doused it in seasoned butter and in another pan started searing a tuna order.

This was it, her time to finally realize her potential. To prove herself. Nothing would stop her. It wasn't solely for her sake anymore, but for the sake of her son, too. She couldn't fail. She was a single mom with a baby boy to take care of.

"Order up!"

The rest of the evening, Shelby managed to keep up with the incoming orders, though still totally thrown by seeing Conor. While she cooked, her mind went over how she'd wound up here, back home in Sandpiper Beach, living with her mother, working at The Drumcliffe Hotel's restaurant.

They'd made a promise their last weekend together, and she'd planned to honor it, too…until her life had imploded.

By Conor's reaction earlier, it was clear he hadn't forgiven her for standing him up. Could she blame him?

"Order up!"

She'd had a chance to study in France three years ago. Hadn't he always told her to go after her dreams? Stuck in another lateral-movement sous-chef job, she'd felt Paris was an opportunity to break out, to finally focus on becoming a renowned chef. While there, she'd met the most talented chef she'd ever worked for. He was *très européen* and sweet and sexy and… How many more adjectives could she use for him? He'd deserved them all.

Of course, she was young and still dumb and she'd let herself get swept away by his amazing charm, his culinary greatness, his *everything*. Most important, he'd made her feel special, like she'd felt no other time in her life.

Wait, check that, there was that July in Sandpiper Beach when she'd felt the same. Loved, cherished, adored. By Conor.

But things soon changed with Laurent. The shine to their romance wore off. The veil slowly lifted from her eyes, and after several months of having her as his chef groupie, he'd gotten bored. She sensed it before he'd told her so. Though brokenhearted at first, she'd tried one last time to make things right between them. Laurent welcomed her back, too. That last night hadn't changed a thing between them. Yet it had changed every-single-thing else.

It had taken moving back to New York, and several weeks, to finally figure out she'd never loved him, that she'd only been infatuated. By the time she'd come to her senses, she remembered the one person she'd loved since high school, Conor Delaney, and how they'd made a promise to meet again. She'd checked the calendar and bought her ticket, deciding not to let anything keep her from the one true love she'd ever known. She'd go home tomorrow, stay with her mother and surprise him on the day. Just like they'd planned, she'd meet him on Sandpiper Beach at the second lifeguard tower. Their lifeguard tower. At sunset.

She'd been packed and ready to go, but something troubled her: her period, or lack thereof, and she couldn't ignore it another day. So she'd taken *the test*. Then fallen on her bed and cried until her eyes burned and face hurt.

There was no way she could fly to California to face Conor as they'd planned. She was pregnant.

By the end of the first evening as head chef of The Drumcliffe, Shelby had cooked and plated nearly a hundred meals. Not bad for a newbie who'd started a stove fire only a couple hours earlier.

There was something else she'd realized. Earlier, when she'd looked into Conor Delaney's eyes, she'd known without a doubt she'd hurt him to the core. That drove home the point how unworthy she was for a good guy like him, when she'd so easily been seduced by a player's charm.

But she still owed Conor an apology, and the truth. Hell, she'd owed him that for over two years, when she should have used her ticket and flown home anyway. It would've been the right thing to do. But she'd been too messed up to face him then, had felt too guilty. Couldn't bear the thought of owning up to one more mistake while feeling so raw and vulnerable. Now he'd find out soon enough anyway. Who knew? Maybe Mark had already told him.

After cleanup and shutting down the kitchen and restaurant for the night, Maureen came in.

"I just wanted to congratulate you," Maureen said. "I've heard so many raves about your food. I'm positive word will get out."

"That's great." Normally, she'd be thrilled to hear it, but Shelby's mind was elsewhere, and she couldn't lay her head down on the pillow that night without confronting Conor.

Shelby and Maureen walked together out of the kitchen. "Can you tell me where Conor lives? I need to talk to him," Shelby asked, just before they turned out the lights.

Maureen looked puzzled. Surely, she knew how Shelby had hurt her son.

"He still lives here in one of the family suites at the back. I just saw him at the hotel pub. But now might not be a good time to talk to him. I'm a little embarrassed to say he's been drinking."

* * *

Conor finished his second beer and ordered a chaser. "Whiskey, please." His second cousin, Brian Delaney, grandson of Grandda's baby brother, Néall, and the new bartender straight from Ireland, raised a dark brow above intense blue eyes.

A bony ancient hand, cold like ice cubes, came out of nowhere and patted his forearm resting on the bar. From the feel of it, Conor wondered if his eighty-five-year-old grandfather was still alive.

"Are ya sure, lad?"

"I've only had a couple of Guinnesses," Conor answered defensively.

"And you have a whiskey, you'll be skuttered. What might be botherin' you?"

Conor resented his grandfather stepping in and telling him to slow it down. If he did that to all his customers, Padraig's Pub would go broke. But he also knew the old man cared about him. Truth was, he had to work tomorrow, and having a hangover wasn't something he needed. Or wanted. "Brian, make that a glass of water." He remembered he'd also had a beer with dinner, so he'd already gone over his personal limit.

Why did he have to remind himself about dinner—the best meal he'd ever had—and seeing *her*?

"Have something on your mind?"

"Nah, Grandda. Just had a surprise earlier, that's all." A surprise that nearly knocked him on his ass—seeing the girl he'd known since fourth grade and loved since the tenth.

Padraig Delaney wedged himself between the guy sitting on the stool next to Conor and his grandson. Far too close for Conor's comfort. "A little birdie told me about the new chef."

Conor had never told a single person how Shelby had stood him up the night he'd intended to ask her to marry him. The man lived in blissful ignorance where his grandsons were concerned, and seemed to like it that way. Grandda couldn't possibly be heading in that direction. "What about it?"

"That Mark hired Shelby Brookes to help our restaurant compete in town."

"Well, from the meal I had tonight, I'd say he made a good choice." He'd do his best not to give himself away. Even though he intended to personally ring Mark's neck for hiring the one person he never wanted to see again. If Grandda had a clue how messed up seeing Shelby had made him feel, he'd start spouting Irish jibber-jabber about the fates and fairies and how life always worked itself out, often in mysterious ways. The Irish version of fortune cookie sayings.

"It's your turn, you know."

Conor almost spilled the water Brian had just delivered. Grandda wasn't really going there, was he? Tonight of all nights? He held up his free hand. "Don't say it. Please."

"We can't deny fate."

There it was. *Give me strength.* Was it too late to reorder the whiskey? But there was no arguing with the man from Ireland with a head full of fanciful thoughts, as his father called them.

"You boys saved that seal. How much proof do you need that it was a selkie? Both your brothers have found their ladies."

Last year, worried about Mark moping around for so long after being discharged from the army, Conor and Daniel had rented a boat for some deep-sea fishing in an attempt to cheer him up. They'd wound up coming upon a pod of orca giving a lesson to an orca calf on how to catch a meal.

The pod had singled out a seal and were wearing it down, giving the calf ample opportunity to do the final deed. Nature was cruel, and the sight disturbed the three brothers. They pulled their boat closer and revved the engine, disrupting the pod's attention. Probably the dumbest thing they could ever do, considering a small fishing boat wouldn't be able to withstand the wrath of a ten-thousand-pound killer whale. But they'd done it, and amazingly, it had worked. They'd distracted the pod long enough for the seal to make a break. As they'd made a wide circle around the pod in the boat, they'd even cheered on the seal.

The next night, when they'd told the family the story over Sunday night dinner Grandda got weird. He'd sworn they'd saved a selkie and according to Irish folklore she—how his grandfather knew the sex was beyond Conor, but nevertheless—*she* owed them all a favor. Grandda swore each of the Delaney brothers would find their mate, as though he had a direct line to the little people in magic land.

Because Padraig was old, and they all loved him, the family put up with his occasional fantastical stories, but this one had gone beyond the pale. Until Daniel met a woman and fell in love three months later, a woman who was now pregnant and ready to give birth. Mark had done the same a couple months after that, met someone right across the street, coincidental as it was. Eerily so?

Nothing like flaming a fairy fire!

Speaking of fire, he remembered the reason he was sulking at the bar—seeing Shelby in the hotel kitchen. She'd been as upset at seeing him as he was with her, and her hand had slipped and she'd started the fire.

As she should be, out of guilt for standing him up!

From the corner of his eye, he saw the pub door open and a woman in a chef smock step into the bar. His palms felt on fire and anxious waves licked upward toward his neck. Seeing Shelby once today had been enough. "Well, I've got an early day, Grandda. I'll be going now." He worked to sound normal, feeling anything but. "Oh, add this to my tab, okay?" He stood and, moving as quickly as possible through a crowded pub without drawing attention to himself, he headed for the back exit.

Shelby swallowed the anxiety that twisted her stomach and threatened to make her turn and run back to the hotel lobby, but resisted and stood in the pub entrance waiting for her vision to adjust. Her heart battered against her chest. Conor hated her. She'd seen it in his eyes. Could she blame him? She'd given him a damn good reason. But he needed to know the whole story.

Still dressed in her chef smock, but without the hat, she stood for a few seconds, back against the pub doors, fighting for balance. It was loud with conversations and laughter, and over the speaker system, classic Irish music played, but by current, popular US groups.

She scanned the pub, checking out the long bar first. Movement at the far end caught her attention. The tall man stood and headed the other way. It was Conor. Had he seen her? Did he hate her so much he'd skip out of the bar to avoid her?

Too bad; she had to talk to him.

Shelby followed, sidestepping couples and groups of people to navigate the crowd and find that back exit. Spying the door, she rushed through it and after Conor, who, thanks to his long legs, was halfway across the hotel parking lot already. She didn't stand a chance of catching him, being a full foot shorter, but she wouldn't give up. "Conor! Conor! Wait up!"

She sidestepped a small group smoking by a car.

Conor stopped, but didn't turn. If she thought her pulse had gone haywire before, that was nothing as it rattled her rib cage now, threatening to break out. Nearly breathless, her lungs irritated by the cigarette smoke, she bolted closer.

"You need to know something," she said, fighting back a cough.

Now he stopped and turned, the parking lot light distorting his scowl into something scary. If she hadn't known him most of her life, she might have run the other way, but she kept closing the gap between them. "I had a damn good reason not to meet you that day." She prayed her knees wouldn't give out as she barreled closer.

"And you couldn't tell me then?"

Closer now, it seemed like a wall of frozen brick separated them.

"Not on the phone. No."

"It was more important to make me feel like a complete fool?" He leveled his voice, aware of the group of smokers.

Still, his cold blast sent chills across her shoulders as she took another step closer so they wouldn't have to talk so loud. "I was the fool, Conor. I'd gotten pregnant." She couldn't help the swell of emotion and the water filling her eyes. "How could I face you?" She hated how her face contorted with the words.

His scowl changed. Had there been a hint of empathy in the expression? Or was it disbelief, and justified betrayal that torqued his brows? On a mission, she blinked away the blurry vision, dug into her smock pocket and pulled out her cell phone. "I swear I'd just found out the day before my scheduled flight home. I was in shock, couldn't think straight. I was falling apart, my life had suddenly changed completely. There was no way I could come home." She brought up a picture, took a deep breath and, with her hand shaking, turned the phone his way so he could see the screen. "This is my son, Benjamin. He's two years old."

Conor studied the picture of her pudgy blond-headed toddler, then slowly stared at her.

Speechless.

Chapter Two

Two years, seven months and three weeks ago, on the beach at sunset by the second lifeguard station, Conor had waited for Shelby. And waited. He'd honored the special date he and Shelby had promised to meet on, and felt like a fool as the last rays of light dimmed and the threads of hope unraveled.

She'd forgotten.

Twenty minutes later, Shelby called him, her voice quivery. She'd explained she'd had every intention of coming, swore she had, even had the plane ticket to prove it.

"So why aren't you here?" he asked, mystified by her absence, and furious. So, so furious.

She broke into tears, soon crying hysterically.

His anger quickly turned to concern. "Are you all right? Shelby, what's wrong?"

She worked to recover, sniffing, gasping air, and fi-

nally, on a ragged breath, pushed out the words. "I can't talk about it. It's too hard."

"Just tell me that you're okay. Are you in danger?"

"I'm not in danger, but I'm not okay." She started crying again. "I'm sorry. I couldn't come. I hope you can forgive me." Then she hung up.

Worried sick, he'd sat staring at the ocean, then the phone, then the engagement ring in his hand he'd been ready to give her. *She'd bought a plane ticket.* Hurt to the marrow, as deep as the love he had for her, he would hold off on passing judgment until he'd gotten the facts.

Conor had planned to ask Shelby to be his wife. He tried to brush off the pain, but her not showing up stung like a demon wasp. His stomach tightened to the point of backfiring. He doubled over, heaved and threw up onto the sand, grateful that it was dark and no one could see him. After what seemed like forever, brokenhearted and thoroughly confused, he'd stood and walked home. Vowing to never let anyone make him feel that way again.

But concern wouldn't let up and, ready to interrogate Shelby, he'd called her the next day. She was at work and said she couldn't talk to him. He'd heard the racket in the background, the voices shouting out food orders. She wasn't lying—nevertheless, her avoiding him cut deeper still.

The next day, when he dialed before he figured she'd be at work, the call went straight to voice mail. *I can't take your call right now.*

He finally got the point. She'd dumped him and didn't want anything more to do with him. But why? And why buy a plane ticket if she hadn't planned to come?

What had changed?

After all the years they'd known each other, he'd thought he'd meant something to her. He'd given her the Claddagh ring, a promise ring, in high school. She'd worn it when she'd left for New York the first time. They may have slipped out of touch in the interim but the promise had always been in the back of his mind. Then six years ago, they'd had the most amazing July together in Sandpiper Beach, falling in love. For real.

Sure they hadn't kept in touch as much as they should have since that summer, but life was busy and complicated for both of them. And he'd never made it back east for a visit. But they'd made a promise to meet again. Didn't a guy deserve to know why he'd been forgotten?

Since that day, he'd thrown himself into his job, dated lots of women to help him forget her, and moved on. Or so he kept telling himself.

Now here he was in a dark parking lot, looking at a digital picture of a toddler, while Shelby expectantly waited for him to say something. As if this situation was normal. In any way, shape or form.

"Cute kid."

That was the best he could offer under the circumstances. An avalanche of pain, confusion and forgotten love crashed over him. And burned. Anguish and aching had been so deep he'd lost himself for a time back then. It'd taken months to feel semi-normal again.

Back in that hotel kitchen, she'd successfully reopened his wounds simply by showing up. Over two years late.

Finally, as painful as it was, he looked at her. The girl he'd known since fourth grade, with the same brown eyes—the eyes he used to get lost in—and light brown hair—though it was shorter and big city stylish now—the same girl, yet so different. She was a career woman now. A mother.

Tonight, face-to-face in a parking lot, thousands of miles still stretched between them. He was a deputy sheriff, he knew how to add things up. She'd said she'd bought her plane ticket, then didn't meet him, and by the picture of her son, the timing seemed about right.

"Thanks." Her reply was nearly inaudible.

His wasn't the response she'd expected from the reaction on her face, a mix between fading hope, agony and facing cold hard facts—there was no fixing what'd gone down between them. Surely she understood that.

Looking resigned, she took back the phone, her fingers cold and trembling. No doubt it'd been hard for her to run after him and show him the reason she'd stood him up. She'd been with someone else and had forgotten to clue him in.

Yet she'd bought a plane ticket. And she wasn't a liar. He had no reason to doubt that at some point she'd intended to meet him.

"I'm sorry, I really am." The mouth he used to dream of kissing again quivered as she spoke.

He could only imagine what'd been going on in her world for the last two years. What had happened couldn't be changed, a little pudgy boy proved it. She'd moved on, hadn't honored their promise like he had. That was the risk of encouraging someone you loved to follow their dreams. Those aspirations had led her away for good. Maybe his father was wiser than he'd thought when it'd come to interfering with his mother's dreams.

He couldn't make his throat work. Didn't try to speak. So he nodded a silent truce, and she nodded back, then he headed for his room, leaving the new chef like a statue in the parking lot watching him go.

Great new menu or not, he'd be eating elsewhere from here on out.

A week later, Shelby was still getting familiar with her routine as the new chef at The Drumcliffe Hotel. Though she'd never get used to that haunted and angry flare in Conor's eyes when he'd appeared in the kitchen her first night. And later in the parking lot, when he'd given her that icy cold stare. She hadn't seen a hint of him since then. He'd been her friend since fourth grade, she'd never get used to the fact that he hated her.

At least she had a job.

Hitting the farmers' market early, in the park just off Main Street, pushing the umbrella stroller with Benjamin happily jabbering to himself, Shelby walked the booths, purchasing fresh herbs and vegetables, putting the items in tote bags hanging over the stroller handles. She wanted The Drumcliffe to serve free-range, local and sustainable meat and fowl products, too, and had to rush back to the kitchen for the latest delivery.

A sheriff's car drove by, prompting a memory of a certain sweet and sexy deputy sheriff—Conor.

"This was the best summer of my life," Conor said, cupping Shelby's face.

"I wish it didn't have to end."

She wanted to cry at the thought of walking away from him again. The last time she'd only been seventeen and she'd had a dream of going to culinary school in New York. He'd given her a Claddagh ring, and foolish as she was, wearing that promise ring, she knew they'd be together one day. Now she was twenty-three, with a new job lined up back east, still on her quest to work her way up to running her own kitchen in a big city. Catching a break in the Big Apple was far harder than she'd imagined, and she was just starting out. She couldn't stay in Sandpiper Beach. No matter how tempting Conor Delaney was.

"Don't let anything keep you from your dreams." His penetrating blue eyes seemed so sincere at the airport.

He was sending her away again. Why didn't he want her to stay?

"I'll call every week," she said.

And she had for the first few months.

"Sure, and once I find a job and get a vacation, I'll fly back to see you."

I'll stay if you ask me. Just say the word.

She stared at her feet, hopeful he might say something. Instead of asking her to stay, he lifted her chin, gazed deeply at her, with something sparking in his baby blues. "Remember our promise. Even if we fall out of touch. Let's meet at sunset in four years." The second lifeguard station on Sandpiper Beach. He'd even verified the day and date on his cell phone again.

They'd spent much of the summer—in between making love every chance they had—pretending to be well-adjusted adults with plans and responsibilities. Look how we've grown up, *they'd silently bragged through their actions and carefree days. Though love simmered just below the surface, the way Conor vehemently insisted she go back to New York, Shelby had been confused. He'd said he loved her, but didn't ask her to stay. At least he'd asked her to meet him in four years.*

If she believed in dreams, and she did with all her heart, then their love affair would survive, and they'd have a fairy tale meeting in four years.

She'd promised to meet him, then they'd shared the most romantic kiss of her life.

Too bad he hated her now. She could never hate him, they'd been friends since elementary school. But she'd have one heck of a job if she wanted to win back his trust. Was it even possible?

Benjamin squealed. He'd seen a parrot in a cage. "Birdie." She pushed the stroller closer so he could see the bird, then checked her watch to see how long before they needed to get back to the kitchen, wishing she had more time to play with him.

At the end of her super busy days caring for Benjamin and since taking on her role as head chef of the small kitchen at The Drumcliffe, she barely had energy left over for anything beyond brushing her teeth and crawling into bed.

Finished with her shopping, she put Benjamin in his car seat and drove through her hometown, struck with how quiet it seemed. There was no traffic noise, no honking or verbal abuse on the streets. So different from New York City. Here, she could hear her own thoughts, and memories of good times in the friendly beach community and the cozy, quiet little town she'd always taken for granted kept returning. Now she longed to fit back in and have a routine, something she'd never achieved back east. *I used to run along the beach every morning.* Maybe if she got up early enough, before her mother left for school, Mom could watch Benjamin and she could take a run? Like the old days. She was too young to think in terms of old days and new days, but being a single mom had straightened her out about her prior carefree life. It didn't exist anymore.

Neither did dreams. She'd lost one too many jobs in New York, and was back home in small-town Sandpiper Beach to regroup. Not exactly the path to culinary greatness.

Reality was a real snotwad. She sighed and turned her thoughts determinedly to the next chore on her agenda, meeting the chicken delivery man for tonight's menu.

When she parked in the hotel lot, she saw Conor's car. The guy who'd taken her to the airport and kissed her goodbye, reminding her about their promise before he'd sent her away. The promise she'd broken. The hair stood on her arms. What if it was his day off and she saw him today? Would it be as horrible as last Saturday night? Nothing could top that out-of-control reaction. She'd nearly set the kitchen on fire!

Whatever pain or sadness she'd caused him, not to mention herself, was history. She was all grown up now with her boy on her hip to prove it. Using her keys, she opened the hotel kitchen—her kitchen—and forced a smile. She was head chef somewhere. Then Benjamin kicked his sturdy legs to get down, but no way would she let him run around her kitchen grabbing anything at his eye level. Soon he quit squirming and pointed through the glass door.

"Truck, I know," she said.

He had a funny way of pronouncing *f*'s instead of *t*'s and she didn't want to encourage him to say *fruck* in public.

The delivery man had arrived with chicken breasts, thighs and legs for today's special, fresh from a local farm.

As she signed off on the delivery from the back steps of the kitchen, Conor left his hotel room, looking dressed for the gym. The pen nearly slid across the page. He looked nothing short of a superhero in shorts and a tight T-shirt. Gorgeous. And to think he used to only have eyes for her.

A memory of their summer together—their bodies tangled tight, with him inside her—made her cheeks heat up. That had been one *hot* summer. *Dream on. He hates you, remember?*

The man would never want to get involved with her again, especially now that she had a son. So why was he in her thoughts at random moments like this?

Because she'd never realized how much she'd loved him until she'd lost him.

* * *

Conor worked out like a madman at the gym, doing double the usual sets on free weights. He'd just seen Shelby again, with her son in her arms, on the back porch of the hotel kitchen, and he needed to get her out of his mind. Sweat ran down his forehead and made his eyes burn. He started in again with a one-armed preacher curl.

He'd been twenty-seven the day she'd forgotten to show up, and he thought he'd never get over her. He'd seriously thought his life had ended for a while there. What a chump. But he'd finally moved on, had even thought about getting engaged early last year.

He transferred the dumbbell to the other arm and started the same routine.

The experience with Shelby had turned his formerly outgoing self inward, and the couple of relationships he'd ventured into since she'd dumped him had failed. No woman wanted a guy who never communicated. Elena had been the unlucky person who'd paid for Shelby's carelessness.

He dropped the weight and stood, pacing the mat while his arms burned and fingers tingled.

He couldn't let Shelby hold him back another day, especially since she'd clearly moved on, being a mother and all.

He glanced around the gym. Maybe he'd ask out the first girl out who showed any interest. With great effort, he remembered his smile and plastered one on while catching the eye of a tall, fit redhead. She smiled back.

Ten minutes later, failing at casual conversation with a willing woman, and having zero interest in asking her on a date, he headed home to shower. It really ticked him off that now that Shelby was back, he couldn't get his mind off her. *Dude, you have a serious problem.*

Once back at the hotel, when he got out of the shower,

he found Mark in the hotel suite. His brother spent most nights with Laurel these days, and it had been ages since Conor had seen him alone. Now that he worked the front desk, Mark dressed in navy pants and a pale blue shirt. The combination made his already deep blue eyes borderline electric. Right now, those eyes watched him. Conor and Mark were overdue for this talk.

"Why'd you hire her?"

"Shelby?"

"Who else." Conor threw the used bath towel on the corner of his bed and stepped into his boxer-length briefs.

"I needed a chef, she applied, she had the best credentials." Defensive as hell. "Aren't you over her? You almost got engaged to what's her name last year."

"Elena. Her name was Elena." Conor pulled on a T-shirt, his back still wet.

"Maybe if you'd brought her around more, I'd remember."

He let that slight roll off, though it was true. "It would have been nice to have a heads-up. That's all I'm saying."

Blue eyes nailed him with a challenging stare. "So I'm supposed to consult you on all things 'hotel' even though you personally told me you didn't want anything to do with running the place."

"It's Shelby, man." On went the jeans. Zip.

"So you *are* still hung up on her."

Conor got in his brother's face. "I can't exactly avoid her since I live where she works. She probably thinks I'm a total loser." He lived there to save for the Beacham House up the coast that'd been sitting empty for years. Like his heart.

He used to want The Beacham for Shelby, now he wanted it for himself. Only himself. A place where he could brood without his family watching his every move.

But even a run-down, never-finished house had to be saved for.

Mark took a step back. "Okay, so you're definitely not over her."

When Conor saw her that morning, it verified his hunch from the other night—she was thin. Too thin. Like maybe she'd been sick or something.

Why should he care? "Beside the point. She doesn't give a rip about me." Hell, she'd obviously been involved with someone else, while knowing about their promise *and* the plan to meet. On the other hand, being fair, which he really didn't feel like being, he hadn't asked her to be a monk, just to show up in four years. *And she'd bought a plane ticket.* "Did you know she has a kid?" It must be hard being a single mother with a kid to support. Maybe that was the reason for the physical change. Stress.

"Yeah, that's why she came home. Whoever knocked her up didn't stick around."

"Hey, show some respect." Like Conor should care how Mark referred to his chef.

"I'm just stating the facts. She and the baby are living with her mother."

Again, why should he care? Maybe because long before they were lovers, they'd been friends. She'd also been the first girl he'd ever trusted. And loved.

Now, he'd never be able to trust her again.

Mark snapped his fingers near Conor's face, getting his attention again. "So you *do* still care. Right?"

Conor gave a frustrated headshake over the density of his brother's brain.

Sunday morning, Conor borrowed Daniel's Labrador retriever, Daisy, for an early-morning run on the beach. Saturday night, he'd broken routine and had gone to The

Bee Bop Diner to grab a hamburger on his way home from work. No way did he want to see *her* again at the hotel.

He needed to clear his head before work, had lost far too much sleep all week and was still completely thrown by Shelby Lyn Brookes turning up back home. On Friday when Mark had come by his hotel room, he'd said she was living with her mother.

Obviously, she needed a place to live. And Mark had given her a job. What happened in New York?

Again, why should he care? Hadn't she slid into the "girl he used to know" category?

The ocean sent angry waves crashing on the rocks, and the sun already promised to heat up the day, even though it was late March. He inhaled the scent of seaweed and briny sea spray to help rejuvenate his confused mind.

By the end of high school, Shelby had been as much a part of his life as his family. During their senior year, they'd spent as many hours as they could steal in a week together. She'd even joined the Delaneys for dinner every Sunday night. He'd cared about her aspirations as much as she'd cared about his. They'd been each other's own private cheerleading team. Now they were just a couple of people who lived in the same town.

Daisy shot up the beach, where further ahead some scrawny kid jogged. Keeping up with Daisy's breakneck pace, he cut the distance between him and the jogger, then realized who it was: Shelby. There went that jolt through his chest again, like sticking his finger in a socket. He thought about turning around and heading the other way, but couldn't take his eyes off her. She might call that gaunt look big-city chic, but to him, Shelby had changed.

What had happened to her? Well, he knew about the pregnant part now, and the kid, but what else?

She'd broken his heart and thrown so much away the

day she hadn't shown up. Yet after all the anger settled down at seeing her last Saturday night, he'd come to face the fact they'd also shared a lifetime of friendship, and, keeping it real, he'd missed that. Heaven help him, he still did.

He kept running, growing closer by the stride. Soon he'd overtake her, and how weird would that be for him to buzz by and blow her off?

The day she'd called instead of showing up, she'd fallen apart on their short phone conversation because she'd just found out.

He slowed his pace. Hell, she worked for his family. He couldn't go on avoiding her forever.

As he jogged and drew closer, another memory from their good old times slipped around him and, without thinking, he cupped hands around his mouth. "Hey! Wait up, Slim!"

Her head pivoted, her body turned. Even from ten feet away he saw the flash of insecurity in her eyes at the sound of his voice and their inevitable meet-up. *Did she still care?*

She let him catch up. "Hey" was all she said. He nodded.

They ran slowly, side by side toward the dunes. Their breathing aligned and her legs worked extra hard to match his long strides. This was probably the dumbest thing he'd ever done…besides making a promise to meet someone years later and actually expecting things to work out.

"I've gotten into a rut," she began out of the blue, capturing his full attention, because until then, the silence had been killing him.

"And this has to do with?"

"Slim. You called me Slim." She slowed to nearly a walk. "And I'm saying I got in a rut somewhere along the way of feeding everyone else before me." Catching her breath, she glanced at him tentatively. "Goes with the territory of being a chef."

He gestured to keep running, then nodded for her to keep talking, too, but she didn't, so he picked up the conversation "So stop that."

She tossed him a confused glance. "Feeding people? It's what I do."

"Leaving yourself for last."

Now she was the one to pick up speed. "Sometimes in the restaurant business, that isn't an option."

"The Drumcliffe isn't exactly a high-end restaurant. Maybe you'll catch a break now that you're home." Oops, from her reaction, he'd ruffled her feathers.

"Running a kitchen is a big job, no matter where." Defensive as hell. "It's just a tough pace to keep up."

"I get that." And speaking of pace, he slowed and motioned for her to turn around with him, heading back toward the hotel. "I'm merely suggesting you feed yourself first, *then* everybody else. If you pass out no one can get fed, right?"

"I haven't so far."

"My mom wouldn't appreciate you testing out that theory in her kitchen, either."

"I know, I already tried to set it on fire."

Finally, she gave up the defensive act, even cracked a self-deprecating joke. They laughed briefly and ironically as they jogged along. Daisy decided to check out Shelby, sniffing in all the usual spots, presumably checking to see if she was female, even while they ran. Shelby shooed her away after patting the dog's head.

He'd started off on a random topic and somehow managed to rattle her cage. A knack.

But things didn't feel nearly as awkward as Conor

thought they might. In a way, they'd managed to pick up where they'd left off on the old-friend scale. But the rest, the ex-lovers part, would be a topic for another day. After running a long time in companionable silence, they approached the path back to the hotel and something crazy popped into his head because he'd called her Slim. Being around Shelby had always set off nutty ideas.

"Let me buy you breakfast."

Out of breath, she looked surprised, like she needed a reason. Like she was the last person on earth he should ask out to eat. "I should go home and shower. Get ready for the brunch."

"Come on, let me buy you breakfast." His inept way of offering an olive branch. "It's still really early."

She stared at him for a few breaths, while he worked on getting used to being around her again. She still rattled him.

"But you hate me," she said.

"I don't hate you. I'm mad as hell at you, and don't know if I can ever forgive you—" he lifted his finger "—but, I don't hate you."

"Well, that clears things up." She glanced out toward the ocean, at her jogging shoes covered in beach sand, then at her watch.

His crazy idea wouldn't let go, and Shelby had just run several miles, she needed to eat. "Remember the place we used to get burgers at? The Bee Bop Diner?"

"That crazy little place that can't decide whether to be a fifties diner or a fast-food joint? If The Drumcliffe job hadn't come through I planned to apply there."

"Seriously? Then you probably already know they serve a mean all-you-can-eat breakfast. Cheap, too. Come on— my treat." He didn't touch her, couldn't. Not yet. But he started up the pavement, then turned back. "You coming?"

"Okay," she said, looking like she'd just witnessed the apocalypse.

Over pancakes and eggs, his guard came down just a bit. Surprisingly they were both hungry and didn't let old emotion get in the way of enjoying a good meal.

They'd been friends long before they'd fallen in love and messed everything up. To clarify, *he'd* fallen in love and *she'd* messed everything up. But they still managed to have a civil meal together. Because they were adults now, right? *Right.*

"So you've got a kid."

"I do. And regardless of how that came about, he's a joy." She smiled, her face softening with the mention of her son. "Hardest thing I've ever done in my life, but I wouldn't trade him for anything."

That certainly set things straight. The boy was first in her life…as he should be. Still, he had a million more questions on that topic that should wait for another day. "He is cute. He's got your eyes."

"Thanks." Her expression spoke a thousand feelings—relief, appreciation and sweetness being the first to pop in his mind.

He might be mad as hell at her, but old habits died hard. "Let's hope he doesn't inherit your height, too."

"Hey." She knew well how to pretend offense at his chronic teasing.

Their eyes met briefly, and a reminder of what they used to have, how they used to behave around each other, stood out. He looked at his last pancake, suddenly full. But he needed to keep the conversation going, even if he was afraid of what he'd hear. "So what's it like to work in a big New York kitchen?"

She sighed, pushing the last of her scrambled eggs around her plate. "How do I describe ordered chaos?"

She put her fork down, her eyes sparking with enthusiasm. "It's like a group dance, semi-choreographed, but with pots and pans, and noise, oh, so much noise." She found the straw wrapper on the table and rolled and unrolled it. "Being part of a kitchen crew is always an accident waiting to happen, tempers ready to flare, insults waiting to get flung." She glanced at him, and as she sensed his interest, her eyes latched onto his. There went another jolt straight down his chest. "And at the end, a miracle, the food gets plated like a work of art, and everyone loves each other again." She lifted the straw wrapper to her mouth and blew to make it unfurl, then laughed lightly. "In other words, it's crazy. Completely nuts. But I love it."

"The meal you served me was incredible."

She dipped her head. "Thanks." After popping a bite of pancake into her mouth, she drank some coffee. "It's got to be nuts being a deputy sheriff, too. Right?"

"Some days. Yeah."

The waiter refilled their coffee cups and removed a few of the finished plates from their table.

"These days with those tragic stories around the country, it's got to be extra hard on you." She looked sincerely concerned.

"It's all in the training, I think. We're into community policing around here, and for a small town like Sandpiper, that works."

"Didn't you work in San Diego for a while?"

"Yeah, right out of college, I got in their peace officer training program."

"I bet you've seen it all." Did she look awestruck?

"I've been in some tough situations, that's for sure."

"Wow. I think you must have the hardest job in the world."

"Hardly, but it keeps me on my toes." For an instant,

he let himself feel *all that*. Why not, she was laying on the compliments like extra mayo on a club sandwich. He puffed up his chest just a tiny bit. Pride went darn well with pancakes. It also came before the fall. "Do you remember how we met?"

Her eyes popped open like she'd just been asked the million-dollar question on a game show, or a security question for a forgotten password. "Grade school?"

"Fourth grade, when you were a pipsqueak." It was his turn to play with the straw wrapper. "And you know why I liked you right off?"

"I thought you couldn't stand me."

"That's because you were the only girl who could beat me at tetherball." Suddenly thirsty, he drank from his ice water. "You had the heart of a lion. That's what I noticed."

From her expression, he knew he'd impressed her, but the big question was why did he want to? Maybe it was carb overload madness from all the pancakes and syrup. Nevertheless, he went on. "You bothered the heck out of me, but you fascinated me, too."

"Then why'd you treat me so mean?" she said with an incredulous stare.

Something about her brought out the tease in him. "Maybe it was your Pippi Longstocking braids."

She covered her face, doing her best not to blush. He could still embarrass her.

Her coffee-with-cream eyes drifted to her runner's watch, then went ultrawide. She looked at him, panicked.

"Oh, my God. Forget the shower. I need to get to the kitchen to start brunch!"

Chapter Three

Shelby and Conor rushed through The Drumcliffe kitchen doors smack into a kitchen crew rushing around, setting up food stations, and Maureen Delaney, with an obviously anxious expression on her face.

"I'm so sorry, Mrs. Delaney!"

"It was my fault, Mom."

Maureen's concern shifted to quizzical, with one curled brow. "I was getting worried."

"I forced her to have breakfast with me," Conor continued. Shelby ignored him, instead focusing on everything she needed to prepare in less than an hour.

Grabbing a chef coat from a hook in her cubbyhole, she shifted into gear. "Did everyone see the menu I posted yesterday for today's brunch?"

Mumbles and affirmations sifted through the small group. "Who's assigned to eggs and making omelets?"

Martha raised her hand. "Do you need help getting your veggies chopped and diced?"

"I'm good," Martha said, dicing bell peppers as she answered, a stainless-steel bowl of chopped onions beside her.

"Conor, can you help her plate all of the options? The avocados are over there, and don't forget grated cheese, sour cream and salsa."

"Sure." He stepped to the basin and washed his hands, impressing her with not having to be told.

"Fred, you're the meats guy, right?"

"Already started the pork chops, sausage, bacon and ham." Of course he had, she could smell the rich, hunger-inducing aroma before she'd crossed the kitchen threshold, even though she'd just stuffed herself with Bee Bop Diner pancakes, bacon and eggs.

"Great, thank you." Relief swept over Shelby as the buffet shaped up. They could do this. Maybe brunch wouldn't turn into a calamity after all, and the teamwork would save her from getting another strike on her record. She needed her job!

"Can someone put together the fruit salad? Oh, and squeeze the orange juice?"

"I can do that," Maureen chimed in.

"Oh, you shouldn't…"

"I enjoy getting my hands dirty. Always have. Don't worry."

"I can help, too," Abby, the head server, looked enthusiastic about pitching in.

That left Shelby to prepare today's special, the peach-stuffed French toast. She bolted to the pantry and pulled out the extra thick bread, threw it on her station counter near the large, long grill, then strode to the double-door refrigerator for a couple cartons of eggs and some cream.

On a second trip, she grabbed the extra-large stainless-steel bowl of fresh peach slices she'd had the foresight to leave overnight infusing in her special mix of spices and natural juice. The preparation smelled great.

The next hour whizzed by as everyone focused on their jobs, and five minutes before ten, when The Drumcliffe Sunday Buffet was set to open, every food station was ready to go. Several times during that hour, Shelby glanced up to Conor's reassuring smile. He knew his way around the kitchen, probably from growing up at the hotel. Even Maureen seemed content with the fare and how the well-orchestrated disorder had all turned out. "I've got to try that French toast," Maureen said.

"You've earned it!" Shelby plated two half slices oozing with the lightly stewed peach sections, and ladled warm maple syrup over the top. "Let me know what you think."

After one bite, Maureen let out a sigh of ecstasy. "Oh, my God, this is delicious."

Shelby grinned and glanced to the right in time to see Conor's proud expression. They'd all worked as a team, focused on one thing and one thing only, to make a damn fine brunch buffet for the hotel guests and locals looking for a change of pace on a Sunday morning. What could have turned into a catastrophe had become triumph.

The action was nonstop for the next two hours. Along with great reviews on the French toast that totally boosted her pride, a few mishaps were averted, and meals kept rolling out the whole time, until the last guest was served and cleanup began.

"I think that's a new record for Sunday brunch," Maureen said, tallying up the server receipts. "Wow."

"Fantastic." Conor offered a high five, and she obliged.

After a brief smile, she got down to business, taking back full responsibility for running the show. "Conor and

Maureen, please don't stick around for cleanup. We've got it covered," Shelby said, glancing at each of her staff.

"Are you sure, dear?" Maureen said, sounding more like a mother than a boss.

"Absolutely. It's a beautiful day, go out and enjoy it."

"Yeah, Mom, go set up your easel and paint somewhere."

"Well, you don't have to ask me twice to do that." Maureen's Mona Lisa smile reassured Shelby that, thanks to Conor taking the blame and sticking around to help, she'd saved her job. Inwardly, she let out a huge appreciative sigh.

Nothing could hide the completely satisfied smile she flashed at Conor, who stood across the room, ready to tackle loading the industrial-sized dishwasher. Was he staying on to help anyway?

The hero points kept adding up, but he'd always been that kind of guy, as far as Shelby was concerned.

A pang of guilt twisted her smile into a near pout. She'd really screwed up where he was concerned. If she could only find a way to make up for that.

If Conor kept staring at the small but mighty chef, her brown eyes flashing with victory, he might do something stupid. Like pick her up and swing her around. So he forced a look at the mile-high stack of plates and the job at hand. They'd been serving too fast and furious to attempt keeping up with washing the dishes during the actual brunch hours.

Something had changed since that moment this morning when he'd considered turning around and running the other way when he'd first seen her jogging on the beach. Over breakfast, things had gotten familiar, like old times, when he could trust her with his life.

The problem was, he'd also trusted her with his heart,

and she'd put it through the food processor. Bottom line, he couldn't get sucked in by her contagious never-say-die attitude, and that great grin. Nope. Too much had changed. Right before his eyes, her smile quickly changed into a lemon-sucking pucker, as if she'd read his mind. She turned and scraped her grill as though removing barnacles from a boat.

She was a mother now, the sole breadwinner for her and her son, who, because of him asking her to have breakfast with him, could have put her job in jeopardy. He was positive, after talking to her earlier, that she still had plans for making it big in the culinary world. Something that was theoretically impossible here in Sandpiper Beach.

Rinsing used to be his favorite job when he'd been coerced into helping in the kitchen during summers. Now, he got a little overaggressive with the hand sprayer on the stack of dishes he rinsed, and soaked his shirt.

She'd only stick around long enough to get back on her feet, then head off to set the culinary world on fire. No way would Sandpiper Beach ever hold on to her. Hell, that was all she'd ever wanted to do since her mother used to barter tutoring for after-school cooking classes for Shelby. She'd told him time and again how that first Little Chefs class had changed her life. From fifth grade on she'd found her calling. He'd been the lucky recipient of hundreds of gourmet lunches throughout high school, too. Back then he'd been her biggest encourager.

Right out of his life.

He stacked another rack of plates on the conveyor heading for the high-temp sanitizing dishwasher, then shifted to the other end. The first batch passed through the splash guards and hit him like a sauna square in the face and chest. He remembered to put on thick, elbow-length rubber gloves before removing the cleaned, and extremely hot, dishes.

They'd had a good run earlier, followed by a great morning and breakfast together, before jumping into save-the-brunch mode. With the extra help from him and his mother, they'd made up some time, too. It'd been fun to be part of her team, and she handled things skillfully, like a trouper. She was a natural on her turf in their restaurant kitchen.

It was the personal level he couldn't handle. Or trust, trust for the girl he'd once promised his heart to. Yet something seemed to have changed between them today. His anger had dialed back a notch. If he didn't watch out, he might get stupid again.

And for that reason, he'd avoid her. It wasn't because he was a coward, he was just being practical. Things had changed, and what they'd shared would never be the same. Once all the dishes had been washed and put away, while Shelby was distracted with her staff discussing Sunday night dinner, he took off.

Wednesday morning, after working out at the gym, Conor stopped off at the local market for a few things he liked to stock in his hotel suite: milk, microwave popcorn, beer, mixed nuts, whatever else struck his fancy. Just his luck, Shelby was there with the kid from the picture on her cell phone, coming straight down the chips and cookies aisle. Benjamin, was it?

Sandpiper was too damn small. So much for avoiding her.

"Hey!" she said, smiling wide, like all had been forgiven, and looking cute in faded jeans rolled up to her calves, with a short-sleeved white eyelet shirt. The dangly turquoise-beaded earrings caught his attention, too.

She also wore beach sandals and her nails were painted bright pink. So like her.

Whether worn out from his intense workout or from holding a long-term grudge, he wasn't sure which, but his animosity had subsided. Back in the day, she was the person he'd known better than anyone else. Never in a million years could he have predicted the curveball by the name of Benjamin.

"What's up?" he said, faking a casual response as he caught her checking out his cart.

"Needed more diapers and milk, but you know how things go at the market." She glanced in her own shopping cart, filled with at least ten other items beyond the two she'd mentioned.

He hid his smile.

"Been busy? I haven't seen you around since Sunday."

So she'd noticed he'd been avoiding the hotel kitchen and dining hall.

Time to fudge. "It's been real busy at the department."

Benjamin looked at him like he was a giant stuffed bear whom he wanted to hug. "Hi," he said to the child out of obligation, never expecting the huge smile he received in return. The look messed with his standoffish attitude, making him want to smile for real, but he tucked it inside.

"I guess that's how it goes in your line of work," she said, making excuses for him, and continuing the small talk. She still managed to get under his skin. Her hair shone under the market lights, and her fresh look, with only wearing mascara and lipstick, appealed far more than he would've liked.

"Yeah, all depends on what's going on in the county." Lame and boring answer, but he wasn't here to socialize, just to grab a few things and get home. He tore his gaze away from her and concentrated on her son, instead—the smiler with big blue eyes and blond curls.

She gave an extra-friendly and overly understanding smile. "Well, if you give me a heads-up any night you're working, I'll have your dinner ready in advance."

"Kind of you." He couldn't avoid looking into her eyes and wondering what else she hinted at. Did she want to see him more? Wouldn't it be easier all the way around to leave that chapter of their lives behind and move on? Something he was still working on.

"Well, you've probably got a lot to do before work, and I'm holding you up," she said, clearly resigned to his resistance.

"As do you." Could he sound any stiffer? They used to be lovers. Maybe that was the problem, he remembered too much. Now his ears felt warm. He'd blame it on the workout. *At least try to be sociable.* "Wouldn't want that ice cream to melt." He chose the most obvious item in her cart, besides the huge bag of diapers, to comment on.

"No," she said, lifting her brows, her mouth in a tight straight line. "Someone told me I needed to feed myself before I fed everyone else, and that's exactly what I intend to do with that rocky road ice cream."

Finally he let a genuine smile out. "Wouldn't want to get between a woman and her ice cream." After her requisite laugh, he said, "Well, guess I'll see you around." Then he politely moved his cart down the aisle.

Thank goodness that was over.

Except when he got to the parking lot, where she was busy putting her boy in the car seat and her groceries were still sitting in the cart. He rolled up beside hers and since her trunk was popped, without being asked, he put her reusable grocery bags inside, then quickly rolled both carts to the corral. By the time she stuck her head out of the back seat, he was almost to his car.

"Thank you!" she called out.

He waved without looking back, because he was going to have a hard enough time forgetting those dangly earrings and pink toenails without seeing her another second.

Shelby sat behind the wheel of her car, staring at the parking lot asphalt. *Stick with the plan. Sandpiper is only a detour. You can't waste ten years of your life. Prove you can run a kitchen, then move on. Go for the goal.*

Conor had worn gym shorts and a snug T-shirt to the market, and looked substantial and appealing. *Okay, say it—gorgeous.* Was she that shallow?

Of course there was more. Conor tugged at every emotion she had. She may have loved and lost him, but there was something they'd always be. Or should be. Friends. Now all she had to do was convince him.

"And where were you last Sunday night for dinner?" Grandda came out of nowhere, maybe from hiding behind the gazebo? Conor was speed-walking back toward his room to cool down, cutting through the hotel side yard, after an early Sunday morning run. Grandda had his interrogation mask on, where he narrowed his eyes until they were slits, and supposedly made the interrogee shake in their boots. At least that was how it used to work when Conor was a kid. He also wore his signature gold golf pants and a bright green vest over a yellow plaid short-sleeved shirt in readiness for his daily game. It wasn't like Conor could pretend he didn't see him, so he slowed down, and his grandfather paced beside him.

"Let me think, that was several days ago. Let's see…" He snapped his fingers. "I had to work late. There was a concert on the beach, and too much beer consumed." In other words, the usual drill for a beach town on weekends.

"You know it's our tradition." Not carrying his usual putter, Padraig had his hands in his pockets. "Especially with your cousin Brian being here. I was hoping you'd get to know each other sooner than later."

"He's here for six months on a work visa, plus we're roomies. We'll have plenty of time." Conor glanced at his grandfather's anxious face. "I'll make a point of spending time with him."

"Good. He's only a year younger than you, you know."

"You have mentioned that a few times, yes." Conor needed to level with him. "Work comes first, Grandda, you know that." Grandda didn't know the half of it, and Conor's plan was, after already confronting Mark about why he'd hired Shelby, not to let anyone else in the family, *especially* his grandfather, know how having her around was messing with his head. "And a lot's been going on."

The suspicious gaze his grandfather returned proved Conor hadn't been nearly convincing enough. Maybe he should have sworn Mark to secrecy since he and Grandda were close.

Conor often blamed work when he wanted time alone, but truth was he'd been looking for excuses to stay late and avoid the hotel and just about everyone who lived or worked there. The last thing he wanted to do was answer questions about Shelby. All that had changed now, so the family might as well all get over it and move on.

"… It's off-putting when you skip out on it," Grandda continued, forcing Conor to click back in and pay attention to their conversation. "There'll be no excuses tomorrow night. I might not be around much longer, and I want my family together on Sunday nights."

Oh, he was laying it on thick today, using his death-bed threats and all. The guy was eighty-five, it wasn't like Conor could predict how much longer his grandfather had on earth, but his gut told him the man would make it to a hundred based on orneriness alone. "Okay, I'll make sure to be there tomorrow night." He raised his right hand. "I promise."

"That's the good lad." He gave a bony hug, then released Conor and took off at breakneck pace for Mark, who happened to be passing by.

Whew. Conor was off the hook, for now anyway.

Sunday night, like a good grandson, Conor arranged his on-the-job dinner break to coincide with the family meal. He gathered Brian from their hotel room tucked away in the back on the first floor, and walked him to the pub, now closed for the standing weekly family dinner.

"How're you liking California so far?" Conor asked.

"It's beautiful. I could get used to the fair weather." His cousin fresh from Ireland had a distinct accent, much like Daniel's wife, Keela, and Conor found it musical and pleasing to the ear.

Brian's broad grin also reminded him of his grandfather.

"I've got a couple days off next week, maybe we can do some windsurfing or sailing together."

"'Twould be grand."

He opened the double glass doors and they stepped into the usually noisy bar to find the rest of his family and extended family already there but not seated. The pub closed on Sunday afternoons to allow for the private family dinners. His clan had gathered in a loose group with three or four different conversations going on, from the sound of things.

Conor greeted his brothers, Daniel, the oldest, and

Mark, the middle, and their respective ladies, Keela, who looked like she could deliver any minute, and Laurel. Then he bent to say hello to the little girls, Anna, Keela's daughter, Claire and Gracie, Laurel's twins, then did a quick fist bump with Peter, Laurel's teenage son. Mark's ready-made family. Conor was proud of how his brother, after resisting any responsibility for nearly a year, had stepped up to the challenge of being a stepdad and taking the lead with the hotel. He guessed all it took was the right woman. The thought pinched tight, so he glanced around.

He nodded at his grandfather, who looked beyond pleased to see him, especially with Brian by his side, though now Keela had stepped in to carry on a fast and furious conversation with Brian, far too difficult for Conor to understand with their Irish accents thickening by the second.

He crossed the room to shake his father's hand and give his mother a hug before they all sat down for the meal. His father, Sean, made sure to make the newest member welcome. "Can I pull you a beer, for a change?"

Brian was usually the one doing the honors since they'd employed him in the bar, under Padraig's watchful eye. "Yes, thanks."

The irony with Sunday night dinners, and the secret reason why Conor had skipped out on it last week, was that he didn't want to eat a dinner he knew had been prepared by Shelby, or risk seeing her. It was the plain truth, no matter how childish that seemed.

Mom cleared her throat. "Everyone. I've invited a guest tonight. Someone who spends all her time fixing food for everyone else, and who deserves to spend more time eating."

Conor lost the healthy appetite he'd walked in with.

"Someone who's been an unofficial member of our family for many years," Maureen went on.

With dread, Conor glanced at the petite form appearing from behind his brothers. Shelby was dressed in a cream-colored sleeveless long shell with beige straight-legged cropped pants, and gold-tinted espadrilles. Her short hair cupped her ears and the bangs swept across her forehead, accenting her warm dark eyes. She carried her toddler, Benjamin, on her hip while the ladies oohed and aahed over how cute he was, curly blond hair and all. Her unsure gaze made Conor suspect his mother had refused to take no for an answer when she'd made the invitation. For an instant, he felt sorry for her, knowing exactly how she must have felt getting strong-armed into a dinner with the last man on earth she probably wanted to see on a regular basis.

He pretended a smile, like her presence hadn't fazed him in the least, though agitation swirled in his stomach. Then he made a point to sit next to Brian, who put himself at the opposite end of the table. Grandda wouldn't dare comment about that, not after their conversation about welcoming his cousin the other day. Though Mom made her dissatisfaction known with a pointed glance and a tilt to her chin. He ignored it.

So be it. If they wanted to play games, he'd double down.

As dinner went on, the usual chaos of Sunday family meals overshadowed the awkwardness of taking a group meal with the woman who'd ripped out his heart and moved back to town, rubbing it in his face.

Benjamin let out a squeal and squashed sweet potato in his hair, with some smeared across his forehead. Mom laughed, so did Dad. Even Conor had to admit the kid was cute. Big blue eyes and pudgy pink cheeks ensured that.

When Conor had studied the boy long enough, refusing to let his mind wander about who his father was and what the story could be, he made the mistake of scanning to the chair next to the booster seat. He found Shelby watching him and, as their gazes settled on each other, something popped in his chest. *Not good.* But she gave a smile that could only be interpreted as further truce. How could he not accept it? He couldn't begin to guess the story behind the story, so until he knew, he'd just have to cut her some slack, if only to make his life bearable.

With the last bite of his chicken parmigiana he let go of another small piece of resentment and regret where Shelby was concerned. Which surprised him, but she'd probably had it really tough over the last couple of years. Why make things worse for her now, and what good would holding on to the negative feelings do?

"Brian," Grandda said. "You will appreciate this story. Your cousins Daniel, Mark and Conor once saved a selkie."

That was the excuse Conor needed to get away. He glanced at his watch, then down the table at his mother, who now held Benjamin on her lap. Before his grandfather could start in on fate and why Shelby came home, taking a job at the family restaurant, he'd leave. His official meal break was almost up, and he'd taken all he could in forced proximity with Shelby, and his family, too, for one evening. The group matchmaking business had to stop.

He stood. "Dinner was great, and now, if you'll all excuse me, I need to get back to work."

Before he made it to the door, someone came up alongside him. It was Shelby.

"Mind if I walk you to the squad car?"

She seemed to be bending over backward to get him to talk to her again. Did she really expect him to open up? It wasn't like he could say no, not with his parents and siblings watching expectantly from across the room. "If you want to, sure."

They stepped outside into the cool night, and she shivered. His first thought was to put his arm around her, but he refused. If she wanted to join him, she'd have to fend for herself. He headed toward the beach parking lot and his squad car.

"How long have you been working at Sandpiper Beach Sheriff's Department?"

"Going on five years now."

She scratched her cheek quickly, noticeable goose flesh on her arms. "Mark said something about you being engaged last year?"

His step stuttered, but he continued toward his car. She kept pace. "Not true. I thought about it, but…" The last thing he wanted was for Shelby to see how screwed up he'd become because of her. "We didn't turn out to be compatible." True translation: Elena had gotten tired of him never opening up or truly sharing anything with her, like he refused to do now with Shelby.

"What do you do on your days off?"

"Do you have something specific you wanted to talk about?" They'd arrived at his car and he pulled out the fob to unlock the door.

"I'm just trying to get a conversation going."

Why? "But I've got to get back to work." Still, that stopped him. How *did* he spend his time off work? Or had work become his twenty-four-hour distraction? "Not much. Run. Go to the gym."

"Do you still hike?" She didn't back down, just stood right in front of him as he opened the car door.

"Yeah. In fact, Mom's talked me into leading some nature hikes for the hotel guests on weekends, if anyone signs up and I'm off duty."

"I have tomorrow off and I heard your mother mention you also had Monday off, so I was hoping you'd consider meeting me for a hike tomorrow morning. Say at seven? Remember the trail we used to really like to take to the top of Shoreline Cliffs?" She looked sincere as hell, and it made him completely uncomfortable, or maybe that had more to do with the cold air and the thin fabric of her top spotlighting how her breasts had peaked. He tried not to notice.

"Mark and I recently took that hike. We were looking for Laurel's son, Peter. He'd run off without telling anyone where he was going." The mountain had a 180-degree view of the ocean. "Why, Shelby?" All efforts were currently fixed on keeping his eyes off her chest.

She seemed hesitant about what she should say. "There's something I need to tell you."

Did he really want to know the story behind her pregnancy, if that was where she was going with the lead-in? Or what if she pushed a second-chance angle? No way could he deal with that right now.

After a moment of strained silence, Conor reconnected with Shelby's gaze. She waited expectantly. He could tell it had taken a lot for her to run after him. Now, like he'd done the other day by asking her out for breakfast, she seemed to be working up to some kind of peace offering. Though he was completely unsure about whether this would be a wise decision or not, the silent pleading in her eyes convinced him to listen. She needed to get something off her chest. Whether he wanted to hear it or not, he had a right to know the whole story.

If that was what she was offering.

He glanced at his watch. Constrained by time and the need to get back on the job, he cut to the chase. "Okay. Seven it is."

He couldn't exactly identify her expression as relieved, maybe there was a hint of panic mixed in, but regardless, they'd just made a date to hike tomorrow morning.

"Okay," she said. "See you then."

Now all Conor had to do was not fixate all night on what the "something" she needed to tell him was.

Chapter Four

Benjamin had been fussy when Shelby had put him to bed. He'd been acting up during most of the Delaney family dinner, too. Maureen didn't seem to mind holding him nearly nonstop during smiles and tears. Maybe she was practicing for her first grandbaby, due any day now. It had been a nice break for Shelby.

At 3 a.m. he cried and felt feverish. He was working on his second baby molars, and the first molars had caused a boatload of grief, along with sleepless nights. Holding and soothing her boy with one arm and drawing up the trusted toddler pain and fever medicine with the other, she knew the drill. She'd been a single mother since the start of his perfect little life. Tonight, she was alone again, since her mother had planned a short trip up the coast knowing it was Shelby's one day off.

Once Benjamin had been born, she'd missed too many nights at work and lost her sous-chef job. She'd scrambled and found another part-time job, but had to live with two other roommates to make ends meet. The stress of keeping her boy quiet while the roommates slept, or vice versa, had turned her into an insomniac and nearly given her ulcers. It also lost her a roommate or two or three along the way.

For the first six months of Benjamin's life, she'd felt like a zombie. Yet pride kept her from moving home. She was determined to prove she could handle life on her own while pursuing her dream, so she settled for roommates who were willing to put up with her and Benjamin. Then, at thirteen months, he got his first bout of bronchitis and she lost her part-time job. Out of desperation, she'd contacted Laurent and asked for help. He'd sent her some money, but asked her never to contact him again. He lived in France, and she couldn't afford a lawyer to pursue more help from him. Life couldn't have gotten any lower.

One of the pediatric nurses who'd gotten to know her over the month it took to get Benjamin better told her about a little café that was looking for a cook. The nurse had thought the owner might be willing to let Shelby bring her baby to work with her.

The suggestion turned out to be a godsend. Getting up at the crack of dawn was Benjamin's favorite thing to do, and the grandmotherly café owner even provided a playpen that converted to a bed for his naps. Most of the time, though, she'd used the baby carrier her mother had sent, which allowed Benjamin to peek over her shoulder while she cooked the short orders four hours a day. Her generous employer even provided a tiny apartment upstairs where they could stay for a minimal fee. Then, six months later, Mrs. Greenblatt passed away, and her out-of-state children closed and sold the small and tattered café.

Unable to find another job where she could bring Benjamin, because the cost of childcare was crazy, she was forced to come home…and face her past.

She couldn't expect her mother to support them. She needed to find a job and Mark Delaney had been looking for a new chef. It was either that or apply for another short-order job at the Bee Bop Diner. Long-held guilt over standing Conor up had weighed her down, but she'd needed a job, and coming home was only a detour, so she'd applied.

Now she'd have to cancel with Conor.

As soon as it was a decent enough hour, she'd tell him, so he wouldn't chalk this up as her being a flake again. If she could keep her eyes open that long. Benjamin had fallen back to sleep.

Conor normally loved early morning hikes, but he dreaded this one, since he'd have to face Shelby alone. She'd insisted she needed to tell him something. What more did he need to know other than that she'd gotten pregnant when they were supposed to meet again? When they'd made their plans to meet in four years, they tried to be realistic. Four years was a long time, so they'd agreed it would be okay to date. In fact, in one bedside conversation back then, feeling all sophisticated, they'd decided seeing other people was only logical. Pregnancy had never entered his mind, but he'd agreed to the terms. After all, it was four years, and dating would help them know if they were meant to be together. Or not. Her having a kid changed everything.

So where did that leave him today? He'd agreed to go on the hike, but he could still call with some lame excuse and cancel. How could she possibly protest when she'd done it to him? Truth was, the less time he spent around her the better he'd feel.

He reached for his cell phone, even while chiding himself for being a coward, just as it rang.

"Conor, it's Shelby." Maybe she agreed with his line of thinking. "Benjamin woke up with a fever earlier and now his chest is congested. I'm sorry, but I'm going to have to cancel."

The hotel chef position offered health care, but she'd only just started and things like that took time. "Sorry to hear that. Does he need to see a doctor?"

"Yes. I'll have to take him to the emergency room, I guess."

So her medical care hadn't kicked in yet. From experience as a law enforcement officer, he knew the best and worst places for medical care around the county. One of the urgent care clinics catered to pediatrics if he remembered correctly from the social workers, where the kids from foster care had gotten great care. "I can give you an address for one of the better clinics, if you'd like."

"Let me get a pen and paper." Benjamin howled in the background. "It's okay, honey, Mommy's going to take care of you." Concern and stress accentuated each of her words, and it didn't seem to soothe Benjamin a bit.

A pang of something he didn't want anything to do with squeezed his chest. "Your mom going to drive?" His mouth didn't get the memo quick enough.

"Actually, she's away today. She knew I had the day off."

Ah, geez. Yet she didn't sound desperate, just concerned, and she'd been a mom for two years now. And she wasn't asking for his help, just stating the facts. Wasn't that what he liked—just the facts? Besides, this couldn't be their first time visiting an urgent care. Still, that pang wouldn't let up; in fact it had changed to needling.

Mark had mentioned that Mrs. Brookes had been helping with her grandson's childcare. Bad timing or luck about today, though. The boy's crying was disturbing and the sound twisted around Conor's chest. He could only imagine how Shelby must feel. Alone. With a sick kid.

"Listen, let me take you. It's probably not a good idea for you to drive while you're distracted." *Dude, the "not a good idea" is getting involved!*

"Thanks, but we'll be okay."

There was his out, but she didn't sound the least bit convincing, more like just being polite, and he used to know Shelby through and through. She wouldn't ask for help, even if her house was on fire. But he swore he'd heard a tiny quiver in her voice.

"Stay there, I'm on my way."

Dude!

Forty minutes later, Shelby, Benjamin and Conor sat on a row of teal-colored plastic scoop-styled seats in an out-of-the-way urgent care all the way across town toward the inland mountains. Determined to take responsibility for her boy, she'd fought Conor's offer at first. Now she was grateful he was here. First off, just to be able to find this place, nestled in the hills in what she remembered was the best part of Sandpiper Beach. Second, because having his support made her feel secure. When was the last time she'd felt like that?

She checked in and waited to see a doctor. Shoving the wallet into her purse, she decided she'd work out how to pay for the appointment later. Good thing she was living rent-free with her mom—an arrangement they'd agreed would last until Shelby got back on her feet. In New York, making ends meet had become a losing battle. Thank heavens for her mother and coming home, something she should have done long before now, except she was hardheaded and determined to succeed. Whether he knew it or not, Conor had played a huge role in her staying away. Yet here she was in a pediatric clinic with the very man she'd been avoiding since she'd gotten pregnant.

Probably out of exhaustion, Benjamin had finally fallen asleep. The odd thing was, it'd happened while she was at the front desk registering her son and had handed him off to Conor. The sight sent a chill, the good kind, down her spine. Rather than ask Conor to give Benjamin back to her, she decided to leave her son well enough alone. Why risk waking him up?

Benjamin looked tiny in Conor's huge arms, a sight both sweet and unsettling. Did he have to hold Benjamin like he was made of delicate blown glass? As if he was meant to hold her son, as though he knew exactly what he was doing? Her chest squeezed at the sight of her ex and her baby.

"Any problems?" he whispered when she sat next to him.

She shook her head, not wanting to disturb her sleeping boy. He didn't need to know about her financial woes. She fidgeted in her chair, one foot ticking an impatient beat. Benjamin stretched and let out a huge sigh against Conor's neck. Conor flinched, like the puff of air tickled. She couldn't help noticing how his deep green-blue eyes surrounded by thick lashes—the ones she used to dream about—widened. Was he surprised? Amazed? Enjoying holding her boy? *Don't go there. Conor and I are finished.* But, while holding her son as he stretched, there was the beginning of a smile, the spontaneous kind that he'd only make when he was unexpectedly pleased. And this moment with the two of them would be the perfect time to take a picture. Big man holds precious stretching toddler. Something Benjamin's own father had never done. There went that heart squeeze again, and her nervous foot. Only in an alternate universe, where things and situations were completely different, could her sweet fantasy survive. Besides, this photo op would have to be a mental one, because Benjamin continued to squirm and now cracked open his sleep-crusted eyes, and that perfect moment was already a thing of the past. Just like Conor.

Instinctively, Conor rubbed her son's back, which surprised and, against her will, touched her in a place she'd protected for the past couple of years. Ben settled a bit, as she became restless with memories and forgotten plans. But she knew her boy, this was the calm before the storm, he was waking up. Then he coughed his tight, congested cough, and on impulse she reached for him. But Conor stopped her.

"I've got him. He's fine. Take a rest. Your shoulders must be aching."

Confident. Logical. So Conor. And she couldn't argue on the last point, her shoulders were stiff and tired. So she staved off her first reaction, which was to take her child anyway, and instead smiled and nodded. Only because she trusted him. The realization caused a dry swallow. But seriously, who did he think he was?

Her old friend who wanted to help her, that's who. Weird fluttery sensations whispered through her chest while acknowledging that truth. Maybe all wasn't lost.

Benjamin lifted his head and looked up Conor's neck toward his face, then over at his mother. Seeing her must have been enough reassurance because he didn't tense or cry about being in a stranger's arms. Instead, he relaxed and put his head back on Conor's broad and sturdy-looking shoulder. Her son was already a good judge of character.

She felt his forehead. He still had a fever. "He's had bronchitis before."

"It must've been tough taking care of a baby, working and living on your own."

She inhaled. "Hardest thing ever."

She sensed something soften about Conor. Sympathy? She didn't want his pity, but she wasn't going to lie about being a single mother. There couldn't be a tougher job in the world.

"Benjamin Brookes?" a nurse called from the clinic door.

Shelby stood. So did Conor. She glanced at him. She should take her baby back, but something kept her from reaching for Benjamin. Her baby was content, and Conor seemed perfectly fine with accompanying her into the examination room. So she let him.

An hour and a half later, after the doctor's examination, an on-site chest X-ray and one nebulizer treatment, Conor, Shelby and Benjamin left the clinic with an antibiotic prescription and a noticeable breath of relief from Shelby. Once upon a time, he'd thought Shelby had the heart of a lion, and she'd proved it by beating a guy nearly twice her size in fourth-grade tetherball. Today, he'd been reminded of that while watching her with Benjamin: she was like a lioness with her cub. On guard. Protective. Obviously filled with love. That kid was lucky to have her as a mother. And he'd expect nothing less of the girl he used to know.

"I guess the pharmacy closest to my house should be good."

"Okay," he said, carrying Benjamin.

When they reached the car, she opened the back door, and Conor bent to place the boy in the car seat. Though he got quickly confused with the double harness straps and multiple buckles, especially since the seat faced backward. So much for teamwork. He gave up and let Shelby do the adjusting, snapping and clicking.

"You hungry?" he said while standing back and watching the expert.

She flashed him a look, as if thinking, *Are we starting with that again?*

"I'm hungry," he said in his defense. And not ready to say goodbye. "That's the only reason I'm asking." *Liar.* He'd cut her some slack on her knee-jerk reaction. It had been a long night from what she'd told him, and she had to be exhausted. Which really was why he wanted to make sure she got fed.

"I could use something to eat," she said, a near-confessional look on her face. *Progress.* She wasn't going to fight him on this. Then she glanced at her protesting son in the car seat. "He's probably starving, too." Ah, the truth.

Conor kept his smile inside. "Okay, then, let's do it. We can put in the prescription, go eat, then go back and pick it up after." *Wait a second, what am I getting myself into? Shouldn't I be holding a grudge or something?* He glanced at Benjamin Brookes's pudgy hands and cheeks, at the boy without a dad. No way could he hold a grudge against him. He was a true innocent in their situation. Then he gave Shelby a long, hard look. She'd been rattled by her son being sick, he'd come to her aid, seen firsthand how deeply she loved that boy, how exhausted she was from being up all night. Shouldn't he cut her some slack, too?

The grudge part, he could deal with later.

Looking grateful, she smiled. A smile he'd tried hard to forget ever since she'd stood him up. "Sounds like a plan."

Whatever he was getting himself into, hanging out with his heartbreaker, and all the old feelings she dredged up, would have to get put on hold for now. At least for today.

* * *

Having Conor's support all morning had meant the world to Shelby, and when he held out his hand, palm up, wiggling his fingers, silently asking for her car keys again, she tossed them to him. He'd driven over, why not let him drive back? If she was honest, she'd admit it felt great not to be in charge for a change. Not to mention Benjamin had really taken to having a big strong man like Conor hold and cuddle him. Yes, she'd seen it with her own eyes, and it'd done crazy things to her heart, so she had to believe it.

An hour later, after Benjamin had eaten and played with in equal parts two scrambled eggs, three fresh strawberries, and a whole piece of toast, and Shelby and Conor had spent another breakfast together—far more harmonious than dinner had been at the pub last night—they arrived at her house. She hadn't needed to remind Conor how to get there, either, considering once upon a time it had been like a second home.

She was relieved everything had worked out okay with the doctor, that Benjamin was only in the early stages of bronchitis. She was also extremely tired: she could hardly keep her eyes open. Benjamin had fallen asleep in the car, and if she handled it right, he'd stay asleep so she could take a much-needed nap.

She got out of the car, yawned and stretched. Conor headed directly to the back seat. She dived to intercept him. Only a professional could carry out the task at hand: removing a sleeping child from a car seat and not waking him.

"I'll do it!" she whisper-yelled, then opened the door. Gingerly, she unsnapped and unlocked the straps, slipped them over Benjamin's shoulders, then unthreaded his arms, all while his head flopped sideways. She hadn't been able to bring herself to get his hair cut yet, so she gently brushed his loose curls away from his face. He was noticeably cooler already, thanks to the magic of modern medicine. She pulled him to her chest, his head plopped against her shoulder, then stood. "The house key has a blue dot on it," she whispered. Still Benjamin didn't stir.

Conor caught on and dutifully strode toward her porch, up the three steps, and proceeded to unlock the front door. Just before reaching the steps, she rolled her ankle on a rock or something on the cement walkway. Conor looked ready to pounce, but she caught herself in the nick of time. She tiptoed over the threshold and into her mother's living room, made eye contact with Conor and, with her lips sealed tight, pointed with her head to the door in the corner, Benjamin's bedroom. He opened it and she smoothly danced around him, holding her breath, heading straight for the crib.

Just as she leaned over to place Benjamin inside, his eyes flew open and he straightened up, looking around, wide awake.

Her shoulders sagged with disappointment. So much for her nap. He was awake. Wide awake. In defeat, she glanced at Conor and they laughed quietly together, which felt surprisingly good.

Once Conor got the okay nod from Shelby, he responded to Benjamin's kicking legs and ready-for-anything attitude. "Hey, buddy, you're home."

"Pway-pway!"

Oh, God, he wanted to play. All she wanted to do was sink onto her mattress and drift into the abyss.

Conor reached for Benjamin. "Old Benny here and I have gotten to know each other pretty well this morning. Why don't you lie down and I'll entertain him for an hour or so."

"I can't let you do that."

"Why not? You're obviously exhausted."

"Do you know how to watch a toddler?"

"I thought I might take him for a walk, let him play in the yard or something. You can change his diaper first, though."

She shook her head, relieved, hesitant and hopeful all at once. She trusted Conor, had since elementary school. "Okay, but only because I'm asleep on my feet, and that's not safe for either of us."

After this morning, with Conor coming to her aid and proving to be nothing short of a hero since, she owed him more than she cared to think. And she still hadn't told him all she needed to.

On a whim, before she reached the door, she rushed to his side, got up on her tiptoes, with Conor obliging without being asked by bending his knees, and kissed Benjamin. Then, without thinking things through, she pecked Conor's cheek as well. The innocent act stirred old and confusing memories—his skin, her lips—and she immediately wished she hadn't done it. Hesitantly looking up at Conor, she caught what she suspected was a bemused expression. She backed away, wishing she could take back the moment, not smell the scent of his aftershave. At least he didn't seem angry.

"We should take a rain check on that hike" was all he said, as he and Benjamin left for their walk.

An hour later, still confused over his reaction to Shelby's kiss, if you could call barely grazing his cheek a kiss, Conor delivered Benjamin to his crib. All the morning's excitement had taken a toll on the boy and combined with his prior sleepless night and the fever medicine, he was out cold.

The front door had been ajar, and after a quiet knock,

Conor had let himself in. From the angle of Benjamin's room in the single-story 1930s beach-cottage-styled house, he could see Shelby in her old room, on the bed, sound asleep. A disturbing sight, considering how mixed up his feelings already were about her. He should still be angry, right? Hold that grudge and walk away.

But he'd spent the morning with her, gotten to know her son, who was a pistol even when sick, and some of those resentful barriers had come tumbling down. Then, out of the blue, he'd asked for a rain check on their hike. Stupid. He knew it was a mistake the instant he'd said it.

Here he was, standing in the hall like a fool, watching Shelby sleep. Like he had the right to, knowing he didn't, as an old sensation circled through his chest. Longing for something he'd never have again. Truth—he missed her.

Making an about-face, because what chump shouldn't, he headed for the door to leave. Then, what the heck, he found a notepad and scribbled out the world's dumbest idea—*Meet you at Shoreline Cliffs trailhead tomorrow morning at 7 a.m., bring Benny if you want.*

He was scheduled for the week on the p.m. shifts. If she didn't show for the hike, or if things fizzled out on the interest scale if she did show, he had a good excuse to avoid her after that: work!

A perfect plan. And entirely ridiculous. Because he was playing with fire, even a fool knew that.

The next morning, regretting his stupid idea, Conor headed down the beach to the trailhead. Shelby had beat him to the meeting point, and stood in the grassy dune area with Benjamin in a back carrier, waiting. With his spirits annoyingly buoyed by relief, he waved. Already he was giving her too much power. Hadn't he learned anything?

She also held a loud pink paisley patterned tote in one free hand, looking readier for a camping trip than a three-mile hike. Wasn't that just like her.

"I think you overpacked," he teased as he approached, fighting that good feeling that continued to bubble up over her already being there.

"I brought some goodies." She squinted from the early sun, smiling.

Flashbacks of that expression he'd seen countless times yanked at him. He knew this wasn't a good idea. He took a second to recover, then, closing the distance, focused on Benjamin. The boy wore something that looked like a fishing hat and cool kid sunglasses, and he squealed when he saw Conor. No way could he resent Benjamin for being someone else's son. That onus was all on Shelby. Reality made his jaw tense, reminding him this wasn't just like old times. Everything was completely different now. She'd moved on and come home with a baby…and he'd closed off, emotionally shut down, turned off the lights and pulled the shades. Except for still being angry. The one emotion he could depend on. But for the sake of the kid in alligator-green shades, he'd suppress it this morning.

"Goodies?" Good thing they were going for a hike so he could work off the resentment.

"Yeah, but you have to earn it," she challenged, turning for the trailhead just when he reached her. "Besides, kids always need snacks."

"Hey, it's not fair with you loaded down with all the extra baggage. I've already got an advantage on height."

She turned, giving her signature dirty look, complete with one raised eyebrow, daring him to pick on her height again. He couldn't stop the twitch at the corner of his mouth. "Why not let me carry Benny-boy?"

"I'm completely capable, but if you want to prove your manhood, have at it."

"Like I need to prove that," he said over a forced laugh.

Without trying they'd slipped back into their old easygoing banter. The trick was to not look her in the eyes. He reached for the backpack-like frame, complete with kid, and helped her slide it off her shoulders. Then she helped him adjust the straps for his broader back and waist, and with Benjamin using his feet on the frame to excitedly push up and down, he adjusted his balance.

The lunch tote had a shoulder strap. Shelby crossed it over her chest, and they set off at a leisurely pace, with her leading the way. He tried his best to keep his eyes off her pert butt and natural sway. See? Playing with fire.

A quarter mile in, she stopped and turned to take in the ocean view. "Wow," she said. "Look at those sunrays." She pointed and snapped her fingers as though trying to think of the name.

"Crepuscular." He finished her sentence, reminiscent of old times.

"Yeah, crepuscular." She watched in awe.

The sunrays broke through a thick patch of cumulus clouds. Like a spotlight on the ocean. The sight made him think the Big Guy Himself was sending a message, but what? Stop? Turn back? Think about what you're doing, numbskull?

"Remember the last time—" she said.

"—we hiked this trail?"

"Fourth of July."

"Day after we ran into each other that summer after college." They'd sat on the bench at the top and watched the fireworks display, along with fifty or so other people willing to make the climb for the view. Then they snuck off to be alone, and that was the first time they'd found the house.

He came up beside her, the view and the clouds lessening his tension, but the memories threatening the balance. "The last time I did this hike, Mark and I were looking for Peter."

"Laurel's son?"

"Yeah, he'd taken off without telling anyone, and we were grasping at straws as to where to find him." Staring out at the ocean, he knew he could never live anywhere but here. "He'd caught Mark and Laurel kissing, and, well, you know how that goes."

"Is he okay with them getting married?"

"He is now." Conor gestured for Shelby to continue hiking and they went on awhile in easy conversation, mostly Conor catching her up on all that had been going on in Sandpiper Beach the past couple of years. But leaving out the part about Grandda's predictions for his grandsons.

Three quarters to the top of the trail, Shelby stopped and gasped. She glanced over her shoulder, making eye contact with Conor and pointing. "Look!"

In the distance stood the Beacham House, set back from the bluff, in full disrepair. His gut twisted. He went quiet, refusing to share her enthusiasm.

"The Beacham House!" she said. "I wonder if it's still empty."

"It is."

She waited for some kind of reaction from him about "their" old playhouse, where all kinds of amazing sexual escapades had taken place. His ears got warm, but he refused to show any other response. She didn't need to know he'd been saving up for a down payment to buy the house. She had nothing to do with that anymore. It was going to be his house, and he was going to work his way up to sheriff, and he was going to spend the rest of his life staring at that damn beautiful ocean with those occasional crepuscular rays. Alone? Being around Shelby again made him think living there by himself could be the worst idea he'd ever had.

He ground his jaw and swallowed the notion of that being his only option.

After a few more moments of silent standoff, they continued up to the top of the mountain trail, where someone had placed a bench so others could enjoy an even more glorious view of the Pacific Ocean. Conor let Shelby sit while he stood by with Benjamin on his back. This wasn't a good place to let a little tyke down, especially since one of his favorite games, which Conor had found out about yesterday on their walk, was to run away and play "try to catch me."

She opened her box of goodies and first gave Benjamin a bright orange cup with built-in flip-up straw, and a mini muffin that looked to be in the bran family. He grabbed it instantaneously as though it might disappear otherwise.

"Plo bloche," Benjamin said, getting right down to business, drinking his water and nibbling on the snack.

"Power muffin," she said, like she knew her kid's toddler language. "Thank you?"

"Ta tu."

That was good enough for her. Next she took out a thermos and unscrewed the lid. Steam swirled out. "Coffee?"

"Smells great. Thanks."

She poured them both a cup, offering his in peace and silence. She'd already mixed in cream, the only way he drank the stuff. Mmm. "I made some croissants this morning. They should still be warm."

She handed him one and his watering mouth clued him in how hungry he suddenly was. "Thanks."

"Ta tu," Benjamin corrected, from over his shoulder. Conor couldn't help but smile.

"Jam?"

Apricot. Also his favorite. She remembered. "Sure."

"Jam!" Benjamin liked it.

Shelby put a minuscule sample on his "power muffin," which seemed to satisfy the kid. Conor took a bite, nearly consuming half of his croissant, and his taste buds shot straight to the leftover half-moon dangling above the sea.

After she took a few small bites and sipped her coffee, she set things down, crossed her leg and laced her fingers over one knee. "So, the reason I asked for us to take this hike," she began in a businesslike call-to-meeting manner, "was to apologize in person." Her head dropped, like her lap had become a huge point of interest. "Something I should have done a long time ago."

He thought about stopping her, because it really was old news, over two and a half years ago, but he wanted to hear it. Needed to. So he kept his mouth shut and let her explain her way out of why she'd stood him up that day.

"We'd fallen out of touch, probably mostly my fault," she continued.

"I'd been bad about that, too," he said, willing to accept his part in their slipping apart.

She gratefully acknowledged his comment with a nod.

Silently, he admitted he'd hoped what they'd shared back then was so special that they could just magically show up on one appointed day and everything would be the same. Just like it always had been. Perfect.

But today, logic kicked in. Just show up. Right. Without putting any work into a real relationship, allowing for dating others in the meantime, while leading up to the big day. What kind of cockamamy plan had that been? He'd pinned his hopes on a fairy tale. Like a big dumb dreamer, and had done nothing more than prove his immaturity.

He scratched the back of his neck, the image of an immature, big dumb dreamer hard to swallow.

"Anyway, I'd gotten totally wrapped up with the restaurant world, and the year before, this opportunity came up to go to France. What cook doesn't dream of going to France?" She lifted her shoulders, her palms up, needing him to understand.

Truth was he didn't want to understand. Mainly because it was too hard to see how out of her thoughts he'd been, when she'd been on his mind all the time. He'd held her in a time capsule of perfection, expecting everything to work out when the day came.

Reason loomed again. Had she? Been on his mind all the time? The honesty center of his brain couldn't let him get away with the prevarication. He'd compartmentalized her, let things slide, had dated more than a few women in the interim. They hadn't taken a vow of celibacy that night on the beach, just made a date to meet again.

So why did it hurt so much when she didn't show up? Damn, so caught up in his own thoughts, he'd missed most of her long-winded story.

"—so I got swept up by the wrong guy, and foolish as it was, I thought I loved him." She shot Conor a glance, as if wondering if her betrayal had hurt him all over again. "Before I realized I didn't love him at all. But it was too late. I was pregnant."

Benjamin had finished his water and threw his cup on the ground. Conor bent to pick it up at the exact moment Shelby dived for it. They bumped heads. Hard.

Ouch! Maybe the pain would knock some sense into him.

"Sorry," they said in unison, their gazes locked and loaded with tension, mixed with head pain.

She retrieved the cup and sat on the bench again. He refused to rub his forehead.

"How could I face you like we planned, pregnant?" she pleaded.

He studied his toes, fighting her logic, wanting more than anything to hang on to his pain and self-righteous judgment, but her honesty wouldn't let him. She may have taken the righteousness out of his judging her, but he was still angry. "The way you handled it?" Considering a two-year-old was on his back, he adjusted his first and honest response. "It sucked. Sucked big-time."

"Please forgive me." She stood and took a couple steps toward him. "You're the last person on earth I ever wanted to hurt."

Her coffee-with-cream stare seemed so sincere, and it would make sense to give in, just say, *Okay, I forgive you.* But it wasn't that easy. He'd suffered like nothing else in his life because of her, and she deserved to know how much. "After I waited and waited, you called and didn't even explain why." Emotion roiled inside, while he stuck to the facts. "You just said you couldn't come." He snapped his fingers. "Like that."

"It took everything I had to call you, Conor. Then I fell apart." Her voice cracked on the last phrase.

He was finally getting a look at the truth from her side, and a surge of empathy tripped him up. He fought it, needing to make her understand how it'd felt on his end. "You dodged my phone calls, when I was worried sick about you. You made me feel like I didn't matter. That I didn't deserve to know what was going on."

He'd lashed out in tired old anger and wounded her. Was that his plan? Whatever happened to compassion? Her face contorted and tears streamed down her cheeks and he immediately regretted being brutally honest. But she should know, shouldn't she? How she'd brought him to his knees, crushed his dream of having a life with her. His chin quivered in response to seeing her cry, and he hated the confusing emotions swirling inside but was helpless to stop them. He clenched his fists.

"I was messed up. I was pregnant. I had a job I couldn't quit. I'd blown it and lost my best friend."

Was that all she'd thought of him? He'd planned a life with her. Queasiness settled in the pit of his stomach. He remembered perfectly the night they'd said they loved each other. It was the same night they'd made their date. Truth was he'd been afraid to contact her in the weeks before, afraid to find out if she'd changed her mind. Then it turned out she had.

"Please forgive me, Conor. Please? I still want to be your friend."

Ah, hell, she was out of control, crying, begging, needing to wipe her nose and looking like she better sit down or she'd fall. They'd started out as friends twenty years ago, this was far from where he'd hoped they'd end up. Disappointment whispered through him, along with his old friend, resentment. But she stood there with tears in her eyes asking for his forgiveness, and he'd always been a sucker when she cried.

She'd come home with her head down and a baby in her arms, having to take the job at his family's restaurant. She'd proved she could swallow her pride for the greater good. Why shouldn't he? Their dream had been dead for two years, since the day she didn't show up. Holding on to resentment had dragged him down enough. The only way to get past the lowest point in his life was to move forward, even if it meant just being friends with her.

What could be the harm reverting back, when all the damage had already been done? On a wave of compassion, he rushed toward her to offer support and the napkin she'd given him with the croissant. She grabbed it, wiped her nose, then latched onto him like he was her lifeline.

"Hey, listen," he said, wanting to make things better. "I forgive you. Okay?"

Relief gushed out of her as she used her forearm to wipe a fresh stream of tears. "Thanks."

Shaken and unsure if he'd made the right decision, he accepted her thanks. Holding a grudge had only made him bitter anyway. "Doesn't mean I'm over it, but I can finally understand why you did it."

She gave a sobby half laugh.

"Mama?"

"I'm okay, sweetie." She immediately changed her voice to mommy-tone. "See, sometimes mommies cry, too." She reassured, and out of consideration, Conor bent his knees so she could be face-to-face with Benjamin. She took off the boy's hat and ruffled his hair, pinched a cheek, then kissed him with a *mwah!*

What she'd offered Conor was friendship. Could he settle for that?

One thing he'd learned as a cop was that people would say all kinds of things when they were guilty, to try and explain why they'd broken the law. Maybe his view on mankind had gotten a little cynical on the job, but as risky as it could be, he still wanted to believe Shelby. Give her the benefit of his doubt. He hoped they could erase all the bad parts and start over as friends. He really didn't want to encourage anything more than that, though. In fact, he wouldn't allow more because only an idiot let his heart get broken twice by the same woman. Besides, being an automatic dad had never been on his to-do list. Never even registered. He'd leave that for Daniel and Mark.

Shelby finished fussing with Benjamin, who was happily oblivious to all that was going on thanks to a flock of seagulls circling nearby.

She was the new Drumcliffe chef. He may as well make peace with the fact he'd see her a lot. Kid and all.

Cool fingers cupped his cheeks. Shelby looked earnestly into his eyes. She pulled his face closer. He didn't resist. "Thank you," she said again, just before she kissed him.

Nothing like that peck on the cheek yesterday, this was a kiss. A real kiss. Soft lips, warm breath and all. The kind that made a guy dream. And he let the sensation roll through him, because it had been a long time since a woman's kiss had felt like this. Like Shelby.

A red flag waved frantically in his mind as her mouth continued to wreak havoc with his. She gave 100 percent of herself, as she always did, and he reciprocated, holding her closer, pressing his mouth harder, until he felt a familiar thrill down to his toes. Friends would've stopped long before now. Who did she think she was kidding, pretending they could revert back, when this was anything *but* the kiss of a *friend*.

Benjamin grabbed Conor's ears and pulled them hard, spoiling the moment and bringing him to his senses. He hesitated, but it was hard to deliver a proper kiss with a kid pulling his ears. Shelby played dirty, too, moistening his lower lip with her tongue. Talk about mixed messages. Benjamin advanced to whapping Conor's temples with his palms, and jabbing his kidneys with toddler toes, and he finally made a clean break. Definitely not a kiss between friends.

Chapter Five

Wednesday night, when Shelby got word Conor was in the dining room for his dinner break, she had a crazy idea. Her head had been spinning since they'd kissed yesterday morning. She wasn't sure what'd come over her after her apology and confession. Then she'd pitched the friendship bit, and next thing she knew she'd had him in a lip-lock. And she'd meant it. That was the part that shook her the most. Coming back to Sandpiper was only supposed to be temporary, a year, or two tops. If she hadn't earned her top chef honors by then, she wouldn't deserve them.

The small-town guy she'd thought she'd grown away from still twisted her hiking socks. Thankfully Benjamin had broken the spell and they'd hiked back down that trail in suspicious silence. They'd said goodbye, then both rushed off in different directions.

She'd thought a lot about him yesterday and last night. She'd annihilated his trust in her and it would take a long time to earn it back, if she ever could. But that was as a lover. All she wanted now was to be his friend again. She hoped to start slow and build from there, since she had a lot of making up to do. So as one friend to another she made an executive chef decision.

"Abby, don't give Conor a menu. I'm going to personally serve him tonight's special."

To help draw new customers she'd decided to have one three-course special every week for a discounted price. Tonight's appetizer was scallop carpaccio with fennel served on a shell. She'd gotten a great deal on the scallop shells last week at the beachside farmers' market, and couldn't wait to use them.

Because she avoided cooking veal, she'd adjusted a traditional osso buco Milanese recipe to use chicken thighs instead, which was cost-effective as well. And tonight's special dessert was lemon panna cotta with fresh blueberries in a light glaze. April was the perfect time for a meal such as this.

She knew he was on his dinner break from work, so she'd start him off with an iced tea. "Here." She handed Abby the tea with two of the scallops on shells. "Tell him, compliments of the chef." She winked and immediately felt stupid about it. All the single ladies in the restaurant and around Sandpiper Beach probably had crushes on Conor. Abby probably thought Shelby was just one more.

As soon as the first wave of dinner guests and their orders were under control, Shelby personally plated the osso buco Milanese for Conor and carried it to his table. It wasn't hard to spot the guy in the uniform who sat a head taller than most others, even though he was tucked away in a dark corner of the dining room, leaving the best seats for paying customers.

Wishing she could stop the blush she felt infiltrating

her cheeks, she inhaled and headed for his table, a smile pasted on her face that, to be honest, felt quivery. But whatever, service with a smile was a Drumcliffe house rule.

"Deputy Delaney, here's your dinner." She made a big deal about setting the plate in front of him, nearly taking out the small table candle in the process.

He stopped the candle from toppling, but not the melted wax from dribbling down its side.

"Good save," she said.

"Wouldn't want to start a fire." His teasing eyes jabbed like a sweet version of a sucker punch.

"Wouldn't want to start a fire." She imitated him, then crossed her eyes. "Thanks for reminding me." Channeling her adolescent self was easy around him.

His mission accomplished, he chuckled. Still, he looked surprised about the chef delivering his meal, which satisfied her to no end. "I was wondering when Abby was going to take my order."

"Thought I'd—"

"Surprise me?"

"Yeah, smarty," she said, adjusting her bright blue toque, while noticing how sea blue his eyes were even by spilled-wax candlelight, and how handsome he looked in his uniform. *Friendship! That's all you asked for. You don't deserve, nor should you offer, anything more.*

"This looks great. And that appetizer? Wow. Superb." He gave the A-OK sign.

"Thank you. I'd love to stay and talk, but I see the room is filling up."

"Of course. Word's getting out about our great new chef. Good for you, Shelby."

She sensed his total sincerity. The guy couldn't fake anything.

Though enjoying the heck out of chatting with her old friend—*and ex-lover*—she forced her feet to move. She had work to do, and tonight didn't only have to do with the important task of mending his trust.

Three feet away from his table, she heard his groan of pleasure. He must have started his meal.

"This is amazing, Shelby. Just amazing."

She turned. "Why, thank you." And smiled, and her gaze lingered longer than it should have on his mouth. There was nothing like watching a man enjoy a meal. That was her excuse and she'd stick to it. Nope. Didn't have a thing to do with their recent kiss. Not at all. Just a guy enjoying dinner.

"Chef?" Her sous-chef, Fred, stuck his head out the kitchen door. "Got a little problem."

She rushed the remaining twelve feet toward the kitchen to find out they'd already run out of scallops and she needed to prepare another batch. Maybe Conor was right, word *was* already getting out about great food at quality prices at The Drumcliffe. That put another smile on her face.

Twenty minutes later, Conor appeared in the kitchen. This time she didn't start a fire or knock over a candle. "You seriously have a gift. All that training really paid off."

"You think so?" His raving over her meals came at a time when her confidence had been at an all-time low. She hadn't been able to find or keep a respectable job back in NYC, wound up working as a short-order cook at a café. Maybe Mark only offered her this out of pity, but she savored Conor's compliment anyway.

"I'm going to tell everyone at the department about these daily specials. Get ready for an onslaught of sheriffs and their families."

"Then tell them we discount even more for our men in uniform." She probably should have run that by Mark first, but too late now! Might be hard to feed a group with limited time, but inspired by Conor's encouragement, somehow, she'd find a way. That was if Mark was okay with it.

"Will do. Pretty soon, people will have to wait in line to get into this place. I'll tell the other officers to get in while they can."

"Thank you." It hit like a bolt, that was how he'd always been, great at building her up, encouraging her to go for it, to run after her dreams. Was he hoping The Drumcliffe Restaurant would be a success for the sake of his family's business, or was he trying to lift her up to get her out of town again? She'd focused on that angle herself when Mark had first offered the job and she'd taken it out of desperation. Get a job to pay your way. Get back in the game. Build a résumé. Apply somewhere else, with more prestige. Someplace far, far away...so she wouldn't have to suffer seeing Conor all the time and be forced to remember all she'd thrown away. But since she and Conor were working on being friends again the original plan didn't carry nearly as much appeal.

Old insecurity about Conor always pushing her away under the guise of helping her follow her dream tweaked the special moment between the two of them, from something special to doubt. Exactly what was the man's angle?

Thursday night, Conor met up with a few officers for the week's special. He'd made a point to let everyone know about the great changes going down at the restaurant.

"Come on your days off, bring your wives and families. You won't be disappointed, I promise. It's my second time having the special this week," he said as the three officers walked into the restaurant together. "I'm no connoisseur, not like Captain Worthington and especially not like his wife, but…"

"The local food critic?" another officer chimed in. "She's probably a total food snoot anyway."

A thought popped into Conor's head. *Food critic.* Then Abby appeared and led them to a table by a window this time. He didn't mind getting stuck in a corner on his own, but when he was trying to impress his fellow officers, in more ways than one, he hoped for better seating. She obliged, and after he perused the menu, Conor recommended the week's special—osso buco Milanese, hands down. "Seriously, DiMaggio, it's probably as good as your mama's."

The crazy thought kept coming back. *Food critic.* What if?

Conor had high hopes of getting a promotion before the end of the year, and knew he'd need a recommendation from his captain. Not that his plans could be considered a bribe or anything. The only thing that mattered to his boss was job performance, and Conor thought he'd been giving his all to his job for the last two years, which proved he had zero life outside of work, but still, he dreamed of the possibility of that promotion.

When Abby served the appetizer, it only took one bite to prove to the others that Shelby Brookes was a chef of great talent. DiMaggio even admitted his mother had never cooked anything that compared.

Two bites in on the main course, one of the other officers put down his fork. "Did you know the captain and his wife are celebrating their twentieth anniversary next week?"

"That long, huh?"

"Yeah, they're going on a European vacation for three weeks, too."

Conor did not know that. Shoot, time was suddenly of the essence.

An opportunity had presented itself that could help Shelby *and* him. And he had every intention of taking advantage of it. But first, he should talk to the chef, then the captain.

Shelby knew Conor believed in her, but suggesting they close the family restaurant for a private twentieth anniversary dinner seemed over the top. Even to a hopeless romantic like her. He'd come back later that night, when she was just finishing closing her kitchen.

"Why are you bent on doing this?" She was positive he was keeping something from her.

"He's a good boss. Twenty years married is also a big deal."

"Yeah?" She hung several of her most used utensils on the hooks above the stove. He followed her around.

"Word is they've been going through a rough patch."

"Sorry to hear that." That she could relate to.

"Some of the officers said he's taking his wife to Europe to save their marriage. And I got this idea how to kick off their plans with a special dinner."

She stopped evading him with busywork. "That's very sweet of you, but won't the others think you're just sucking up?"

"Probably, but I don't care."

Was it true?

"Look, the guy guided me from my first day on the job. I've looked up to him, tried to live up to his standards. I'd hate to see his marriage fall apart on account of his job."

The idea of shutting down to the public and doing her part to help save a marriage did ring of romance through and through. And being honest, Conor had a touch of romantic in him, too. Or at least he used to. A quick flash of them having a picnic in front of the Beacham House's fireplace came back. He'd thought of everything including a small vase of wildflowers picked from the nearby hillside.

She leaned against the sink counter and crossed her arms. "Okay. I'm game if Mark and your parents are okay with it. That's a lot of money lost."

"Not if we do it on a Monday night, when the restaurant is closed anyway."

So there went a day off. Was it still worth it?

He watched with an earnest expression as she thought things through. She was the one with a lot of making up to do. If he wanted to plan this one special event for his captain, she'd do her best to knock it out of the park with a special meal. Day off or not.

"Okay, so I'm thinking lobster."

Before she said another word, Conor hugged her. Tight. Then he picked her up and spun her around, planting her feet back on the ground. She forgot all about side dishes and dessert and succumbed to his strong body, so close, and how she'd missed it. Missed him. How he still smelled of lingering lime-scented aftershave and the deputy sheriff uniform eight hours into his shift—a heady stew of secondhand smoke, beach air and someone's too-sweet perfume. That part dished out a huge serving of jealousy, which prompted her to be bold. She stopped short of turning her head and kissing his neck. Someone else's cheap perfume or not, he was still a great hugger.

Unfortunately, he let go, his eyes wild with ideas. "I'll have my mom decorate the room. We can move all the tables out of here except for one." He pointed to the center of the dining room. "Right there under the chandelier."

"The better the ambience, the better the food?" Still,

she hoped that some of the wild in his eyes was because of her.

"Nah, you've got that part nailed." He glanced around the empty dining room, as if imagining exactly how it would look. "Now all I have to do is convince Captain Worthington."

"You haven't talked to him yet?"

"I'm laying the groundwork with you first. Why promise something I can't deliver, right?"

Did he purposely say that to hurt her? "Uh, right." The comment stung regardless, due to the nagging guilt she carried with her every single day.

Things were so messed up between them.

"I've got to take off, track down my brother and run this by him. Now that I've got my chef on board, this might really happen." His enthusiasm was almost contagious. Except for one insecure thought.

Was that how he thought of her, merely as a chef?

Conor wound up working overtime and didn't get home until seven the next morning. He knew where to find his mother, since it was her favorite time to paint. Walking across the lawn to the edge of the beach, he found her with her easel in her usual spot, painting.

"Good morning!" she called to him as he approached, ocean breeze whipping red hair around her face, a Delaney clan plaid blanket over her shoulders.

"I brought you a coffee. Great idea about setting up a coffee center in the hotel lobby."

"Thanks." She took the proffered cup. "On both counts. You just getting home?"

He peeked around the corner of her canvas, and was awed by how his mother managed to capture the sea. This morning, thanks to the clouds and the wind, the painting depicted whitecaps and turmoil. "Yeah. Crazy night. Had to send some officers to the men's colony again, too."

"That's not good."

"A few bad apples riling folks up." Conor made a point of not talking work much with his mother, because it worried her. "Everything's fine." For now. He took a sip of his decaf in hopes of falling asleep as soon as his head hit the pillow. "They needed some extra bodies to stay on in the department."

"Still trying to impress your captain?"

"Nah. You know me, always happy to make an extra buck."

"The Beacham?" Her train of vision moved slowly from her easel to his face.

His mother was the only person besides Mark he'd told about his dream to own the place. He nodded. She returned a supportive smile, then looked back at her canvas to add a few more strokes. His secret was safe with her.

He glanced at the ocean in time to see a wave crash against the rocks, sending sea spray like a geyser. "Hey, speaking of impressing my boss, I wanted to run something by you before I overstep anything and make plans."

"Go on." Her eyes roamed from canvas to sea and back, as she leaned forward and delivered a few quick brush-strokes.

"I'd like to use the restaurant on a Monday night in a couple of weeks for a private dinner for Captain Worthington and his wife. It'll be their twentieth anniversary."

"You mean like a party?"

"Uh, no. A private dinner. Just the two of them."

"A dinner." Her brows rose as she dabbed her brush into the dark blue glob on her palette.

"It's kind of a two-fer. Shelby's agreed to knock their socks off with a meal they won't forget, which is good for me, but also for her. She doesn't have a clue Mrs. Worthington is our county food critic."

"Why not tell her?"

"I don't want to stress her out or put extra pressure on her."

"I think if I were a chef, I'd want to know."

"But that's the point, I've been reading up on this and evidently food critics don't let restaurants know when they pop in."

"Like secret shoppers at the market?"

He'd never heard of that one. "Yeah, I guess," he said, screwing up his face watching his mother deep in painter's mode, her wizened green eyes in total concentration. "Anyway, not that Mrs. Worthington will actually review us, but I thought, in case she did decide to, a good review might bring in more customers. I guess that makes it a three-fer."

"A three-fer, huh?"

"If all goes well."

"And Shelby doesn't mind spending her night off cooking?" Maureen Delaney appeared to be having her end of the conversation with the canvas.

"She didn't even hesitate, well, for long anyway."

"Mark know?"

"He's next on my list. Thought I'd run it by the real chief before I did." He waited for her to look at him, then winked, and she grinned.

"He's doing a fabulous job, and running a whole lot more than you realize. If he says yes, I'll say yes."

"Okay, but one more thing, the food critic part has got to be a secret. No stress. No pressure. No disappointment for Shelby. Just a secret shot at getting a review."

"My lips are sealed."

Conor took one last look at what was shaping up to be another dramatic and beautiful oil on canvas by his mother, a woman whose talent had remained untapped because she'd been stuck running a hotel and raising three boys most of her adult life. It never seemed fair, as far as he was concerned. "That's beautiful, Mom, as always."

"Thanks. I'm determined to have one of my paintings in every single hotel room."

"Great idea. The paintings in the lobby really class the place up."

"Mark's idea." She didn't need to say it, her pride for son number two was evident.

"Okay, then, I'll go talk to him about the dinner." He fought off a yawn, then kissed her cheek before taking off across the lawn for the hotel lobby. "I'll tell him Mom says I can."

He always enjoyed his mother's easy laugh.

Late that afternoon, after a few hours of peaceful sleep, Conor showered and shaved, and headed to The Drumcliffe kitchen to bring Shelby up on the plan. Walking across the parking lot from his hotel suite, he felt something shift inside. An old grudge. The thought of facing Shelby didn't make his gut knot up like it had at first. They'd spent enough time together to help him get past some of the pain he'd dragged around with him for far too long. Old habits, like being friends with Shelby, had come back. So instead of being uptight about it, he climbed the half-dozen stairs and opened the kitchen's back door with an honest-to-God smile on his face.

"Hey," he said when he spotted her stirring some kind of amazing-smelling red sauce. "Looks like all systems are go."

"I know. Mark told me." She wore a bright multicolored scarf around her head, mostly covering her short hair in the back and had tied a knot above the part for her bangs.

She looked vintage and cute, even when she cooked, like something that belonged in a logo.

"He didn't waste any time." Mark had also agreed about keeping the food critic part a secret.

"Neither did you." She smiled, finally glancing up from the industrial-sized saucepan.

Dang, she was pretty when she did that, and it bothered him that he noticed so easily. "You sure you don't mind giving up a day off?"

"It's for a good cause."

She didn't know the half of it. "That's true. Okay, then, I'm going to talk to Captain Worthington tonight."

"You do that."

The only downside was having to turn from her smile and head to the sheriff station.

A few others puttered around the kitchen, so Shelby waited until Conor hit the back stairs to go after him. The sauce could simmer, no worries there. She wanted to talk to him alone, to get something off her chest. The private meal was her ticket to buy back some trust from Conor, but there was more to it than that, and she was never any good at keeping her thoughts to herself.

"Conor?"

He turned with an expectant gaze. "Yes?" And damn, he looked great in his deputy sheriff uniform.

"I just wanted you to know how grateful I am that your family has given me this second chance."

"Well, everyone deserves one. And it was Mark who gave it to you."

She reached out for his arm, lightly stroking down the brown uniform sleeve. Since he stood two steps down, she met his gaze eye to eye. "I can't tell you what a giant weight has been lifted off my shoulders since telling you the truth about my situation. You deserved it from the start. I'm sorry I went a little crazy back then."

"I might have gone a little nuts under your same circumstances."

She squeezed his forearm. "I remembered needing to call you, so at least there was that, but then I froze and broke down, and messed things up even worse."

He shook his head, maybe because he didn't want to rehash that night again. She locked onto his gaze and didn't let go. In her gut, she knew she still had more to explain. For her sake. To help finish cleaning up the mistakes she'd made. She understood she was no longer worthy of Conor's love, but maybe, just maybe she could earn back some of his respect. That was why she'd cook the heck out of the anniversary dinner for his boss. Because words would never be enough for what she'd done. "I'm sorry." With every ounce of her heart she meant it.

"I believe you."

She was thankful that from now on she could focus all her attention on her new job and caring for Benjamin. But secretly, she'd cherish every moment she had with Conor, because her old feelings kept renewing themselves whenever she did. "Thanks." He had no idea how much this meant to her. Or maybe he did.

Something seemed to change in his eyes. She hoped it was trust, and counted it as progress. "Oh, and I'm going to run everything by you for this special dinner. Taste tests and all. So get ready, buster. I won't serve a thing you don't approve of. I want to do my part to save that marriage." Whether the captain's situation was symbolic of theirs or not, she really wanted to give that married couple a second chance.

Now the shift in his sea blue gaze darkened. His hands came to her shoulders and he drew her to him...for a kiss.

Their kisses had been adding up, and each time had grown more intense. Man, this one nearly made her apron sizzle. And it was his idea!

She relaxed against his mouth for a moment before he delved deeper, as though testing to see if there was still anything left between them. Tension coiled inside, and she met his passion with her own, their tongues getting to know each other again. She'd taken his kisses for granted back in high school, then during that amazing summer they'd gotten so much better at it. Right now, he proved he hadn't forgotten all her favorite tricks, and little tingles ran up the backs of her knees.

She dug her fingers into his neck and opened her lips, remembering and loving the silky feel of the inside of his mouth, the thrill of being so close. Tasting him. Inhaling his fresh-from-the-shower scent. Much nicer than the cheap perfume stuck on his uniform the last time.

His hungry kisses contrasted with the tender touch of his hands on her back. He restrained himself, that was clear. Maybe the next time they kissed, he wouldn't? A girl could only hope.

She treasured this intimate moment, reminiscent of so many others when they were a couple. Long ago. All she could do was hope he felt their special buzz, too, because then she might have a chance to win him back. Wait, what part of that had anything to do with her long-term plans? The scary thought made her tense midkiss.

He must have sensed it, because in the next moment, he ended the back porch make-out session, looking as confused as she felt.

"We seem to be doing a lot of this," he said. "Are you okay with it?"

"Kissing you? Always have been, but—"

"We're only supposed to be friends?"

She nodded. "Something like that."

"Is that how you really want it?"

Was it? She'd asked to be friends with him when she thought that was her only option. When she was still sure she'd only stay in Sandpiper Beach as long as it took to find a bigger and better job. Now she wasn't sure about anything, and he deserved an honest answer.

"I'm not sure."

Chapter Six

Conor knocked on the classic Queen Anne front door of the beautifully restored Victorian house owned by Laurel, his soon-to-be sister-in-law. "Is Mark here?" he asked when she opened the door.

"Yes. Come in." The brown-haired woman with kind eyes stepped aside so he could enter the reception area of the B&B. "I'll go get him."

While he waited, he took time to check out the detailed touches she'd added to the stately home. A crystal chandelier that belonged in another era. An amazingly long oak table in a dining room that stepped back in time. He'd been in the house a dozen times, but now was the first he'd noticed how meticulous her taste was. He couldn't keep his mind on his surroundings for long, though, because of a certain red-hot and ragged kiss he'd just delivered to Shelby. His heart still beat noticeably faster. What had come over him?

For one thing, she'd kept touching him, then she'd admitted how much being a part of his life again meant, even if they were only friends. He'd let her explain, for at least the third time, the misguided reasoning of a woman who'd just found out she was pregnant the day she was supposed to fly home to meet him. Didn't make that day hurt any less, but oddly enough, that day and the pain that followed was beginning to feel more and more distant. What did his mother used to tell him? *There are always two sides to a story.*

His big mistake had been looking in her eyes while she squeezed his arm. Her touch had set off buzzing along his skin, even through the cover of his sleeve. Her sweet, sexy gaze had invited him in. As the old song went…and then he kissed her. Now he wanted to kick himself for letting his guard down. No matter how hard he'd tried to shove the feelings deep down, he still wanted her.

He'd tried since the day he'd discovered she'd returned to Sandpiper Beach to make rhyme and reason out of the crazy twist of Shelby coming back to town with a baby. To torture him? To make peace? A little of both? Any which way, the logic evaded him. Now they were supposed to be friends. Just friends. So why did he kiss her like he wanted her the way he used to?

Because he did. The thought jolted him through the floor.

"You look like a troubled man," Mark said, his longish dark hair messy, like he'd been taking a nap or working too hard over a computer.

"You don't know the half of it," Conor replied.

"Is this about the anniversary dinner?"

"Nope. That seems to be shaping up all on its own. I've been thinking."

"Uh-oh." Mark grinned. "Well, in that case, maybe

we should sit down. Can I get you some lemonade?" For a guy who'd checked into a dark place for the better part of a year when he'd first been honorably discharged from the army, he now looked comfortably at peace, here, of all the places, in a traditional Victorian B&B inhabited by three kids. Was that what love could do?

Conor followed Mark into the modernized kitchen. "Sounds good." His throat had been dry since he'd broken off the knockout kiss with Shelby, had seen her steamy expression. But he got completely confused when she'd admitted she wasn't sure what she wanted with him. Hurt, he cut things short, said he had to get to work. To cover for that crazy story, he'd actually driven from the hotel parking lot across the street to here. As if she wouldn't notice.

He sat at the extra-long marble kitchen island while Mark poured the lemonade.

"So what have you been thinking about besides anniversary dinners and secret food critic capers?" Mark passed a glass to Conor, then sat on the stool next to him with his own.

"About Mom."

Mark twisted up his face. "Mom?" Clearly surprised.

"I know, right? But ever since Shelby's come home and I've seen firsthand what a gifted chef she is, I've been thinking she and Mom have something in common."

"Seriously?"

"Yeah, they've got a major thing in common."

Mark canted his head, as though trying to put two and two together. "Too bad you're going to work, because this conversation sounds like it needs a beer and Grandda's pub."

"Or a psychiatrist. I know. A lot has been going through my mind lately." He wouldn't bore his brother with what percentage had to do with Shelby. The amount might shock him.

"And what's Shelby got to do with Mom?"

"Both of them, in their own way, are artists who're trapped in this small town."

"Mom's never seemed unhappy about it."

"Not obviously." He took a drink of Laurel's minted lemonade, surprised how good it always tasted. "Do you remember Grandda ever saying something about how Mom had to make a choice between pursuing her art or continuing on with the hotel and family duties?" Had he been eavesdropping on a personal conversation between his mother and grandfather as a boy? The memory was only clear on the gist of the conversation, not the circumstances under which it occurred or the details as to whether Grandda made the ultimatum or Mom had told him her decision.

"Can't say I do."

"I remember her getting very quiet for a few weeks around that time. Don't you remember something like that?"

Mark shook his head, though looking like he was doing a quick mental scan through his childhood.

"Maybe Daniel will remember." Being the oldest brother, Daniel had four years on Conor, and the difference between an eight-year-old boy and a preteen was gigantic. "Even though I was just a kid, I got the distinct impression she would have liked to have seen if her beautiful ocean paintings were good enough for an art exhibit or something."

"Man, you had deep thoughts when you were a kid. The only heavy thought I remember thinking when I was eight was about frogs and how if I held them too long they peed in my hands."

"Deep." Conor couldn't help laughing at the absurd memory his brother had come up with. Mark shrugged. "But seriously, you never got the impression Mom wasn't happy?"

"I hate to admit I probably wouldn't have noticed unless she'd cried all the time or fought with Dad."

And that had never happened.

"What's this got to do with Shelby?"

"You see how talented she is, right? She had a career that could've gone somewhere back in New York, but she got pregnant. Now she's had to come home and work at our hotel."

"So that's why you're setting up this *anniversary dinner*?" Mark used air quotes around *anniversary dinner*.

"Of course. How else can we get a food critic for the *Central Coast Ledger* to consider a review of our chef?"

"Are you happy she's back or trying to find her a job somewhere else?"

"Well, if you put it that way, I'm not sure." Maybe because of his fears about his mother at such an early age, he'd always wanted the best for Shelby and her dreams of becoming a famous chef. He'd always encouraged her to go for it. "It's just that now, in her own way, Shelby is trying to prove herself as good enough to compete with the finest chefs in big cities. You've noticed her menus."

"Of course I have. She's doing exactly what I asked her to do when I hired her. And you asking her to cook for your boss, whose wife happens to be a food critic, is to help Shelby make a name for herself?"

"She's worked so hard and deserves it. Don't you think?"

"Of course, but we just got a dynamite chef for our hotel and I'd hate to have some power restaurant steal her from us. This was supposed to be about improving *our* business."

He would hate to see that, too, but she was a mom now and had to think about her and Benjamin's future. Staying in Sandpiper Beach, living with her mother, would keep her locked away.

"And doesn't growing up in a small town sound better for her boy than a big city?"

"You've got a point there." So the bigger question turned out to be, was he trying to help her career merely for the sake of her future, or was it to get her out of his life again? Because it was still painful to want more with her again. He glanced at his watch. "Oh, hey, I'm gonna be late if I don't get rolling."

"Yeah, shouldn't be late when you need to ask your boss for a date."

"If all goes well, The Drumcliffe Restaurant will be so busy you'll have to hire extra staff." Or they could lose their chef to a bigger, better opportunity. There went that rock in the pit of his stomach again.

"Wouldn't be a bad thing, would it."

To lose Shelby? "Huh? Oh, needing extra staff? Nope. Then Mom and Dad could retire knowing they'd left the place in your good hands."

They shared a complicated handshake they'd done since they were kids, meant as a family-styled goodbye.

Mark walked him to the door. "I never realized how close to Mom you are."

"I'm the baby, right? Didn't you and Daniel used to call me Momma's boy all the time?"

"Until you grew taller than both of us by the time you were thirteen and we knew when to keep our mouths shut."

The brothers parted with light laughter, but Conor

wasn't anywhere through making comparisons between Shelby and his mother and their unspoken discontent. He'd call Daniel on his dinner break.

"One last question," Mark called from the doorway.

Lost in his thoughts, Conor turned halfway to his car.

"Why does Mom always look so happy, then?"

Conor shrugged—did his mother look happy or was that a mask she wore to hide her disappointments—and continued walking to his car. Maybe Mark thought she was happy because every person saw what they wanted—or needed—to see?

Once Shelby got the word the special anniversary dinner was a go, surprisingly from Mark first, not Conor—whom she hadn't seen since their sexy kiss—she dug through her ingredients lists. Of course she'd stick to seafood being as they were in a beach city, but something told her to go untraditional. Lobster and pork bellies! Yes, that would be the twist.

Now she was excited.

But to be safe, since she didn't know the couple celebrating their anniversary, she'd give a second choice of good old traditional filet mignon.

She'd kick things off with a bang, maybe something with shrimp.

She'd also give two choices for dessert, pie or cake.

With her head spinning with ideas, it was possible she'd change the menu ten times before the actual meal next Monday.

The main thing was she didn't want to take too many risks or get too fancy for a couple celebrating their anniversary in a rough stage of their marriage. When it came to cooking, safe was far from her middle name, but for the sake of not embarrassing Conor, or The Drumcliffe, she wouldn't take any unnecessary risks.

"How are your plans coming?" Maureen Delaney entered the kitchen, evidently straight from her afternoon painting. She wore an old light denim shirt splattered with colors from her palette, and gray yoga pants. She'd also forgotten to take off her large brimmed straw hat, which was obviously for protecting her redhead complexion.

"Great." Shelby was still on a roll with ideas. "You know what I'd love?"

Maureen waited expectantly, brows lifted.

"If you and Mr. Delaney, Mark, Laurel and Conor also participated in this meal. As I serve our guests, you can all eat here in the kitchen, having our own little party. What do you think?"

"Won't that be a lot more work for you?"

"Not really. I don't know how to prepare small, so there'll be plenty for everyone to try. As it stands, I'm making a dual menu in case one or the other doesn't like lobster."

"Lobster? Oh, I'm in. Yes, count all of us in. We can be your cheering section for your big night."

Her big night? "It's just an anniversary celebration, right?"

"Oh, right," Maureen said as if she'd messed up and needed to cover up quick.

But cover up about what?

Maureen's phone rang. "Sorry." She quickly dug it out of her big pocket and answered as if relieved to drop the conversation. "Now? How long? Oh, my goodness. Let me get Sean and we'll be right over." She hung up with wide, excited eyes. "Keela's in labor! Has been all morning. Daniel needs me to bring Anna to Laurel's after school, then we'll head over to the hospital." She rushed toward the door, not giving Shelby a chance to react.

But react she did. Memories of her solitary labor and delivery in New York contrasted with Keela's. A deep sense of sadness washed over her. What must it be like to have an entire family's support? Did Keela know how lucky she was?

Later that night, Shelby needed more booze for the night's special—grilled chicken marinated in tequila. The dish had gone over so well, she had to make more. Everyone was busy in the kitchen, and when she called Brian asking him to bring some over from the pub, he'd told her he was swamped and didn't have any help.

Didn't Padraig pitch in on busy nights, or would he be keeping vigil at the hospital with the others?

She rushed through the front restaurant doors, across the lobby toward the pub, but skidded to a stop. Conor was behind the registration/check-in desk.

"What are you doing here?"

"Keela's having the baby, so I'm covering for Mom."

"Do you know what you're doing?"

He screwed up his face. "Of course. I grew up around this place."

Right. Made sense.

A male guest approached the desk, looking annoyed, so she scuttled on.

"The room card key you just gave me didn't work," she overheard. Amused, she turned to watch the fallout.

"Oh, sorry. Let me fix that." Conor retrieved the card with a pleasant professional expression, and re-magnetized it, then handed it back. Shelby chuckled under her breath over his feigned insult when she'd asked him ten seconds ago if he knew what he was doing.

He could be so darn adorable sometimes.

* * *

After hearing Keela had delivered a healthy baby boy and they'd named him Keiran, Shelby had texted Conor and made an appointment for him to sample her planned menu. Friday midmorning she met him at the hotel kitchen door.

Since it was a weekday and her mother was teaching, and she'd normally be home with Benjamin, she'd asked Maureen if she'd watch him for an hour so there wouldn't be any distractions. Maureen was happy to do so, and also thrilled to show no less than fifty pictures of her new grandson on her phone.

"Hey," he said, seeming a little distant, typical of their one-step-forward, two-steps-back reunion.

She'd stick to the business of feeding people and keep their personal hot mess on hold for today. Or at least that was the plan. "Bring your appetite?"

"Of course." He smiled and she relaxed some.

"Good. Hold on a second," she said. "Let me put this on you." She held a long scarf, doubled it, then prepared to apply it as his blindfold.

"Looks interesting." From his heated mischievous gaze, she secretly wished she was leading him into a bedroom, but stomped on that thought immediately. Too late, the skin on her chest sprang with goose bumps that spread like wildfire to her breasts, and damn, she'd worn a thin top.

"Bend down so I can tie this," she said, trying desperately to sound all business, knowing he'd noticed the state of her nipples.

With what could only be described as a titillated expression, he cooperated. She took his hand and elbow and led him to the restaurant kitchen island where she'd laid out her final menu.

"Something smells great."

After changing her mind a dozen times, she'd stuck with most of her original ideas, but wanted Conor's final say.

She guided him to a chair and helped him sit. The hair on his arms rose from her touch. Suddenly the blindfolded taste test seemed far too intimate. Regardless, she allowed herself to ogle his jeans-clad long legs and tight butt, his gorgeous arms and broad chest thanks to the navy blue T-shirt stretched snug and tucked in. He smelled great, too. How had she ever thought Laurent could compare to Conor?

She took a sip of ice water from the counter to clear her mind, and offered him room temperature water to clear his palate. She also noticed he smiled, like he was enjoying everything.

First she offered a tiny spoonful of two different dressings for the salad. He agreed with her first choice so champagne vinaigrette it would be. She gave him a taste of lemon sorbet to wipe out the acidic taste to prepare him for the appetizers.

Next, she gave him a small bite of the sweet potato puff with chorizo. He liked it. A lot. Which made her smile. After a shot glass of whole milk, she handed him a seafood stuffed mushroom.

"Which do you like better?"

"The mushroom is good, but I like the subtle kick of the chorizo in the sweet potato better."

"Great. Thanks." After some lemon sorbet, she gave him a shrimp-and-mint spring roll, the whole thing since it was small. Part of the draw with that particular appetizer was how it looked in the nearly clear noodle wrapping, but Conor would only experience the taste.

"Wow, that's good. Got any more?"

"I don't want to fill you up too soon, but when we're done you can eat all you want."

"Understandable."

"So that's a yes on the spring roll?"

"Absolutely."

After giving him a plain water cracker, they moved on to the lobster dish. First, she served a bite of the lobster and noodles.

"Oh, my God, that's great."

Smiling, she handed him another shot of milk, then a bite of the caramelized pork belly.

"What is this? Wow, I like it."

"It's pork belly, to contrast with the lobster."

"They're in the same dish?"

"Yes."

"Genius."

She lightly slapped his deltoid, in disbelief, but her heart reeled with excitement.

"I'm serious."

The man never ceased to praise her, and right now she felt like she could conquer the world, not only Sandpiper Beach. Grinning until her cheeks hurt, she gave him another plain water cracker to erase the fatty taste. In all her training, she'd never enjoyed a taste test as much as this. "I'm skipping serving the meat because it's pretty traditional and you've already had my style of steak. But what do you think of this as a side starch."

She gave him a spoonful of fingerling potatoes, parsnips, carrots and brussels sprout, roasted and seasoned with sea salt, thyme and rosemary. Literally holding her breath for his reaction.

"Good."

Only good? "Instead of a traditional baked potato, sour cream and chives?"

"Absolutely. That tasted healthy and should be a compliment to the steak." His hands rubbed his thighs, as though he was totally getting into his role as a food critic.

"You're beginning to sound like a professional." That got a smile out of him, and she admitted that below that blindfold, his smile was sexy as hell.

Not wanting him to know how he turned her on, she modulated her voice. "Okay, well, that should be it for the appetizers and main course."

"That's all? Then feed me more lobster. Or at least a spring roll. My mouth is watering."

He wanted her to feed him. She let her mind wander to the sensual foods she'd like to feed him, if she ever had the chance to seduce him. The best way to a man's libido was always through his mouth. Then she made a mistake. After he swallowed his second bite of lobster, noodles, miso and white soy sauce, with just enough heat to wake up the taste buds, she was overcome with a sudden desire to share the heat. So, she leaned forward and pressed her lips to his. What had come over her?

Him. All of him. That was what had come over her. Being too close. Wanting what she couldn't have. And who could resist a gorgeous blindfolded guy?

She tasted her cooking on his lips, and was relieved when he didn't fight her kissing him. He sat with his hands on his knees, acting like this was a new way to clear the palate between courses. It took all her self-restraint to keep from crawling onto his lap and wrapping her arms around his neck. Instead, she kept the kiss chaste, but full of yearning as she ended it, and a promise for more.

"Can I take the blindfold off now?" he whispered, making her skin prickle again. She basked in the feel of those tingles, wishing things were different between them.

If he took off the blindfold, she wouldn't be able to

hide her warm cheeks and the desire simmering inside. *Let him see.* "Yes," she whispered back.

He pulled off the scarf and studied her, a serious expression in his eyes, making no effort to touch her. If she could only read his mind. Had she blown it, getting so carried away?

"Everything was perfect," he said in a low, sexy rumble.

"I want it to be perfect for—" so wrapped up in their moment, heat centering between her thighs, she almost messed up and said, "for you," but caught the words just in time "—your boss and his wife."

"It will be. Trust me." Instead of reaching for her to continue the kiss, like she'd hoped, he stood and grabbed another spring roll.

"What about the desserts?" Disappointed, she wanted to keep him near, make love to him through her food.

"My mom would be the best taste tester for those." He'd clicked out of the simmering moments before. All business now.

"Okay." She'd blown it by kissing him. "I'm sorry if I—"

"Nope. Don't apologize. Everything was perfect. It's just I've got to go." His no-nonsense tone changed the atmosphere from sensual to tense.

She worried her mouth, wetting her lips, then biting the lower one. "Okay. So everything's good, then?"

"Perfect," he said, glancing from her head to her toes, then back to her face, making her wish she'd worn something sexier than leggings with an extra-long tank top.

"I've signed on for more hours this weekend, to make up for taking off when Keela was in labor, so I probably won't see you until Monday night."

Disturbed by the change in mood, she needed to know. "Is everything okay?"

"Some inmates at the men's colony are stirring things up over there. I'm taking the extra patrol time so the captain can send some manpower to the prison as backup."

So wrapped up in the kitchen menu and her personal thoughts and wishes—thoughts about rekindling something much deeper than friendship with Conor—she'd forgotten the responsibility of his job and how dangerous it could be. The realization sent a shiver through her. "I hope everything works out."

"I'm sure it will. Just part of the job. See you Monday." He reached for her arm and kissed her cheek, then left, leaving her longing for more.

The man was bent on keeping things on a friend level, but had confused the heck out of her by kissing her like old times the other day.

So typical of this one-step-forward, two-steps-back dance they'd been doing since she'd moved home.

The following Monday night, Shelby knocked it out of the park, offering the perfect anniversary meal to Captain Worthington and his wife, Felecia. Conor knew firsthand since he and Mark and Laurel and his parents all enjoyed every course in the kitchen, while the couple had The Drumcliffe dining room all to themselves. Conor also made a point to keep his distance from Shelby, something that grated on her, but she had plenty to keep her distracted.

"She's loving every bite," Abby reported, upon her return from collecting the main course dishes. The desserts were all ready and cappuccinos made, waiting for table delivery.

"I'm so happy to hear it," Shelby said, cutting a couple

more pieces of pie, then on another plate two more pieces of cake for the Delaney clan to share.

But it seemed odd how everyone focused on how Mrs. Worthington liked the meal. Wasn't this for both of them?

Abby had said the Worthingtons had decided to share both desserts, just like they had every course she'd made for the night. "But what about Captain Worthington, isn't he enjoying it, too?"

"Oh, yes, but it's the Mrs.'s opinion that really counts."

Why? Because she was the one unhappy with the marriage? Shelby thought Conor wanted to do this special thing for his boss. Didn't his reaction count? Conor shoved a huge bite of cake into his mouth at the exact moment she caught his gaze with questions on the tip of her tongue.

Things weren't adding up, but she was still thrilled the night had been a success. Exactly for whom, she was no longer sure, though.

"Oh, my Lord, this is delicious." Maureen was the first to swoon over the red velvet cake with confetti bits in the cream cheese frosting that added a celebratory flare.

"Mmm, like sex on a plate," Laurel said, glancing at Mark and then at his parents, her eyes slightly widened, as she blushed bright red. "Also, I need to get some of your appetizer ideas for my B&B."

Good subject change!

"Anytime. We can make plans to meet here in the kitchen and I can show you a few quick, easy, but delish recipes."

"I'm definitely taking you up on that." Laurel smiled before eating another bite of cake and rolling her eyes with the goodness.

Shelby couldn't help but think she could become friends with a woman like Laurel. In fact, each week of her employment, she felt a little closer to the entire Delaney family. Except for Conor, who kept pushing her away.

Padraig appeared at the back entrance to the kitchen. "What's all this? I thought we were closed on Mondays."

"We are," Sean said. "Didn't you get the memo? It's a private anniversary party for Conor's boss. Come, have some food."

"No one said a word to me," he said, looking disappointed or confused. "I just had a sandwich at the pub, but you can cut me a piece of that pie. Tanks."

"Yes we did. I personally told you about tonight last week," Sean said, a touch of worry to his brow.

Was Conor's grandda's memory slipping? Now Shelby was worried, too. She glanced around the kitchen. The only ones missing from the Delaney clan were Daniel and his wife, Keela, but they had a good excuse—their new baby. Plus Brian, who was busy bartending in the pub. A warm and frighteningly inviting sensation tiptoed up Shelby's spine. The group felt like a second family, and she was getting in way over her head. She'd come home to get back on her feet and move on. Then Conor had thrown a wrench in the works by forgiving her and being willing to be her friend. She'd hurt him to the core, and their supposed friendship made him a bit flinch-y, but he was trying. Honorable as always. And lately, running the kitchen at The Drumcliffe, she was finding that her big chef dreams seemed to be landing much closer to home. If only she could make Conor give her a second chance.

An hour later, when the group cleanup effort was finally done, Conor put the largest pots back in their spots on the highest shelves.

"Hey," Shelby said, at his back. "Will you walk me home?"

Mark, Dad and Grandda helped move the tables in the dining room back to their regular places, and Mom and Laurel were loading the last of the dishes to be washed. All looked to be under control, except for his heartbeat. Did he want to walk Shelby home? Yes! Would it be wise? No! Should he walk Shelby home anyway? He wasn't sure. But she'd worked so hard for his personal cause, which also secretly happened to be her cause, so he'd go with his gut.

"Sure. After all that great food, I could use some fresh air."

Felecia and the captain had been so appreciative of the special evening when they'd left, Conor thought his arm might be shaken off his shoulder. Still, it felt good to do something extra-nice for someone, even if there were some ulterior motives and lots of rewards, as in also having a great meal. Who but Shelby would think up lobster and pork bellies over lo mein noodles? Genius!

Mrs. Worthington had also given Conor a meaningful wink when she'd said good-night. "You've got a good chef at The Drumcliffe." She nodded, businesslike, and he hoped it meant she'd write Shelby up for her newspaper column. He didn't dare ask and risk ruining the whole evening. It was their anniversary after all.

The one thing Conor didn't like about heading out with Shelby was the knowing look that passed between his parents. He swore, sometimes they were as bad as his grandfather.

The late April air was brisk and cut through his polo shirt, making him think Shelby must be freezing. He thought about putting his arm around her, then realized she'd come prepared with a hoodie sweatshirt. An odd mix of disappointment and relief confused him, as did all things with Shelby. They walked in companionable conversation. Her going over the meal and how everything came out exactly the way she'd hoped.

"I've told you before how talented you are," he said. "You should be working in some big city where you'd get noticed."

The look she returned was not what he expected. The excitement had left her face and she got quiet.

"I'm just being honest, Shelby."

"But I just got here. Do you want to get rid of me already?"

"Things are different now. You know that."

"I thought what we all shared was different, but in a good way. It felt great to be a part of the Delaney team tonight. Why are you always pushing me away?"

She had the nerve to ask him that? "Me pushing you away? You were the one who didn't show up."

She took a deep breath and attempted to walk faster than him, obviously forgetting how much longer his legs were than hers.

"I'm sorry," he said. "Okay? That was a low blow. I'll stop bringing it up."

"But you'll never stop thinking it. I blew it. I know. I was just kind of hoping that after tonight, especially after tonight, we could start to move past that."

He slowed a bit, and she waited for him to get in stride with her again, a hopeful expression in her eyes. "I can't guarantee anything."

She shrugged. "Well, that's better than a no."

All the good feelings they'd shared for the entire evening had somehow been dragged out of the way, leaving them facing their old and tiring truth. He'd waited for her and she'd stood him up.

Still, something shifted in her eyes. She took his hand and pulled him along for the last block to her house.

"I know you probably would've rather been home with Benjamin tonight, so thanks for everything."

She squeezed his hand as they walked toward her front porch. "I still get to sneak in his room and kiss his forehead and watch him dream, and I get to be the first person he hugs in the morning, too."

The idea of having that with a child surprised Conor. A kid's love had to be the purest form of love, long before all the complications of life set in. He'd found out how forgiving little kids were when he'd babysat for Laurel's twins. All they wanted was him to like them, and anything he did was like the greatest thing in the world. After getting over feeling ridiculous sitting on a tiny chair and pretending to play tea party with them, he'd enjoyed himself.

Shelby pulled him up the three stairs to her front door, then maneuvered him away from the porch light, to a darkened corner. "This is for believing in me," she said, going up on her tiptoes and reaching for his neck, then planting those sweet lips on his.

And they were definitely getting used to kissing again. He reached around her back and pulled her close, kissing her deeper, teasing with his tongue, then wandering to her earlobe for a quick nibble and enjoying her quiet gasp. Memories of how quickly they could catch fire invaded his thoughts. Was it wise to take the kiss to the next level? Definitely not, but everything about her felt great, great like she always had, and he couldn't resist. When he kissed her again, his hands drifted to her butt to pull her closer still, intent on letting her know what she did to him. A faint murmur escaped from her throat. It drove the point home, and he balked. He was nothing but a moth to flame, making out with Shelby again. And he was the one bound to get hurt. Not her. Why let history repeat itself?

"I should be the one thanking you," he said, easing up

with his hands, pulling away just enough to use his mouth for something other than making out. Trying not to be obvious. "You knocked it out of the park tonight." Like right now with that kiss.

Instead of kissing him again, she studied his eyes, hers moving back and forth over the bridge of his nose, like she was working up the gumption to say something. It would be easy to kiss her again, but he knew they shouldn't keep this up, that it could lead to her bed. He was the one who needed protecting where Shelby was concerned.

"What do I have to do to win back your trust?" She'd obviously sensed his hesitation, and there was the hint of frustration in her whisper. He owed her the truth and took a moment to give it.

"Erase the past. I can't see beyond that to trust you again."

"You want me to erase my kid?" she blurted, appalled by his statement.

"Not that part, of course I didn't mean that."

"Because he's the whole reason I let you down."

"No, Shelby, you let me down by getting involved with someone and forgetting about our promise."

She dropped her hands from his shoulders and backed up. "I never forgot it. But I did get distracted. I've said I'm sorry over and over."

"And I believe you. For the record, I even like Benjamin. It's just…"

"That I can't erase all the rest. Right?"

With tremendous regret, he had to come clean. "Right."

She pulled completely away. "So you and I are *impossible*."

What could he say that he hadn't said already?

She walked backward toward her door, dug in her

pocket for the key. "Good night. Thanks for walking me home." Then, as quickly as she could, she let herself in.

And Conor stood staring at the door until his pulse slowed down and his weak legs were ready to walk again.

Chapter Seven

It was impossible. Shelby could never win back Conor's trust, he'd said so just now on her front porch before she'd left him standing in the dark. Which meant any hope for a relationship was lost.

After checking in on Benjamin in the tiny sewing room now turned into a toddler haven, and saying good-night to her mother, who was reading a book in bed in the master bedroom, Shelby fell on her mattress and cried. Silently, so her mother wouldn't hear. Mom could never stand to see her sad, and boy, *was* she. Tears streaked across her cheeks and pooled on her pillowcase. Coming home and facing the man she'd left behind had been the second scariest part of her life, after having a baby in a big city all by herself. She should've come home immediately when she'd found out she was pregnant, maybe she could have prevented this whole fallout, but she'd been headstrong and determined to handle her mistakes by herself. She'd expected Conor to understand.

Wrong! And what was she thinking, that he was perfect or something?

She shook her head—she may have made some humongous mistakes, but she'd never think of Benjamin as being one. He was the best thing to ever happen to her. More tears flowed over the sorry circumstances since returning to Sandpiper Beach.

She should be riding high from the success of the night—the anniversary dinner was near perfection. But Conor had managed to rip away the dream that mattered most. There was no way to erase the past. It'd made her who she was today.

Unable to sleep, she turned on the light and, wanting to find a few of the memories she was supposed to erase, decided to rummage through her old closet. Mom had kept so much of the stuff she'd left behind.

She had to push the wooden desk chair into the definitely-not-a-walk-in closet, to reach the shelves where several boxes had been placed. Architects didn't plan for much closet extravagance in the kind of 1930s California bungalow she'd grown up in. But after living in New York for the past ten years, her bedroom and closet felt like a palace, and she didn't even have to share the small room with her son.

She pulled down the first long plastic-lidded box, put it on her bed and rummaged around inside, only to find old report cards dating all the way back to elementary school. *Are you kidding, Mom?* There were achievement awards—probably every single one she'd ever received—term papers and projects, art projects from when she was five. She laughed. On and on. Underneath it all she found a stack of school class pictures, from first grade and up.

In the sixth-grade graduation picture, her being short, she stood in the front row looking ridiculous with bangs nearly covering her eyes and straight hair long past her shoulders. It was almost blond back then. Two rows behind her was Conor with the tall kids, and he towered over everyone. She'd recognize those eyes anywhere. He looked cocky and confident and she seemed completely dorky. It made her laugh, remembering she'd regularly beat him at tether ball. It was all in the angle when hitting it, and for once her being short was the advantage. Man, he had to have taken heat about that from his super jock friends.

On to the next box, which had an abundance of baby items, and since Benjamin was a boy, she didn't spend much time with that box. The third box had more of her personal things. Old diaries. Wow, she'd forgotten how diligent she'd been about telling her various diaries everything going on in her life, like it really mattered. Again, she smiled, holding one in bright pink covered in white hearts close to her chest. She didn't dare open it because each and every one after the age of ten would have focused on Conor Delaney, the "man she'd marry one day."

An ache centered in her chest. Talk about lost dreams. Her smile quivered and more tears flowed.

At the bottom of the storage bin she found an eight-by-ten wooden box with a lid that fit imperfectly. Like something made in wood shop, which she'd never taken, preferring to use her class electives for the few cooking courses hidden in the family and consumer sciences department way back in middle school. Even then she knew what she wanted to be. On the back of the unevenly stained box, the letters *CD* were carved. Conor Delaney.

As her heart got infected by the ache in her chest, she inhaled the scent of the musty wood and memories rushed through her. Maybe it was from crying, but her head went woozy with those thoughts. He'd given it to her in eighth grade, the year they'd first tried out kissing. Her fingers fumbled to open the box, only then remembering what she'd deemed special enough to keep inside. A wallet-sized picture of him in tenth grade that was signed, "Love ya, Conor." Suddenly she channeled the moment he'd given it to her, and how thrilled she'd been. That summer she let him feel her up, not that there was much to feel, but man, he seemed really excited about it.

More grins, wet ones, along with the mixture of feelings coursing through her. Old innocent times, when she lived safely tucked away in her town and school. Like a snow globe, but of the beach. The hardest part of her life had come early when her parents fought all the time and eventually got divorced when she was eight. Those were sad times, but she and her mother had made the most of it. And though her father had cheated on her mother, she'd never bad-mouthed him in front of Shelby. Though she'd eavesdropped on many of her parents' heated phone calls, and remembered being scared. Like she and her mom might become homeless or something without Dad. She'd sworn that when she grew up and loved someone, they'd never argue like that. As she got older and learned the truth about her parents' divorce, then firsthand experienced her father's disinterest, she formed her own opinions about the man. About men in general. She hadn't gotten the kind of dad she'd hoped for, and Benjamin wouldn't have the dad he deserved. That was how life worked.

Dear Diary, Conor would never be that way. She'd distinctly remembered making an entry or a dozen like that years later when she'd first started crushing on him.

A few special letters and birthday cards were bundled together, many of them from Conor, and… *Oh, my God!* The ring. The Claddagh ring he'd given her in eleventh grade was in a tiny black velvet drawstring bag. She picked it up, turned it around, remembering the special meaning. It was delicate as a glass wing butterfly, and it wasn't just the silver braiding, or the design, with the crown, heart and clasping hands, that made it so special. The meaning extended all the way to which hand and what direction it should be worn. She squinted to remember. In a person willing to consider love with another, the tradition was to wear the ring on the right hand with the crown pointing away from the heart. When he'd given it to her, she wore the heart pointing inward, because that meant they were in a relationship. If the ring was meant as an engagement, it was worn on the left hand, crown pointing out. She remembered secretly wearing it on her left hand when no one was around to see, pretending Conor had asked her to marry him, then daringly pointed the crown inward, toward her heart, imagining how happy they'd be married.

He'd made a big deal out of how his grandfather had helped him choose the ring and that it'd come all the way from Ireland. She wondered why he'd given her the ring when all he seemed to want was for her to move away for culinary school. Probably out of guilt, her father had come through with the tuition. Conor was the one she'd confided in about her plans to become a chef and he got right on the bandwagon. "You have to go, Shel, it's your dream." He hadn't called her Shel once since she'd been home.

She slipped the ring on her right hand, making sure the crown pointed toward her fingertips, since, if memory served her right, that meant she was looking for love.

Conor had held his breath when she'd taken the ring from him and first put it on. Of course she'd pointed the crown toward her heart on her right hand. They were in a relationship, making a promise to each other, because once they graduated everything would be guaranteed to change in both of their lives. She was going east and he was heading south.

He'd given her the ring a couple weeks after they'd gone all the way after having both been virgins. So daring, scary and wonderful to get that close to someone. He'd been as gorgeous naked as she'd imagined. He'd told her she was beautiful, when she felt anything but. Yet there was awe in his gaze that night. Did he still think she was beautiful?

Would Conor even remember the significance of the ring and how it was worn?

A crazy idea came to her. What if she turned things around on Conor. Instead of erasing the past, like he insisted, she'd flaunt it! Force him to remember all the good things about them. Maybe then he'd forget the bad…the part he wanted erased.

She stopped cold. What was she thinking? This wasn't part of her five-year plan. She was home temporarily, only long enough to make a name for herself and gain credentials. Sandpiper was the detour to her dream.

She started to put the ring back in the box, but couldn't. She had a battle to fight. She needed the ring to help win back Conor's trust.

It was Saturday night before Conor ate at The Drumcliffe on dinner break again. He'd confessed his true feelings to Shelby and she'd left him standing in the dark on her porch. He understood it was impossible to take back that night she'd stood him up, even though they'd made a promise and she should have warned him in advance she couldn't make it. And that was still the trouble: he wasn't sure, after all this time, if he could let it go.

Nothing mattered anymore, because he'd admitted the

only way he could forget was to erase the past, and to use her words, that made them "impossible." The last couple of weeks, being around her, he'd made the mistake of remembering how things used to be, but now he'd faced the fact they were impossible, and he was finally ready to move on. But before he cut things off completely, there was something he needed to tell her, before she found out on her own. At least he owed her that.

Why it mattered, he didn't understand, but it did. Felecia Worthington had written a great review in the *Central Coast Ledger* about The Drumcliffe and their new chef. Evidently Felecia had pumped Mom for some personal statistics about Shelby and had included them in the article. Central Coast California would now know much of Shelby's personal business—being a single mom—along with what a great cook she was. Conor wanted to explain his reasoning for not telling her, before she read the paper herself.

He pulled into his assigned hotel parking space and cut the engine. In uniform, he strode across the lot, heading for the back door to the kitchen. He'd noticed people waiting out front for dinner, and thought it better to grab his meal in the kitchen tonight.

He pasted a smile on his face, wanting to be upbeat about the good news that could help Shelby's career, though remembering how they'd left things on the doorstep the other night. She'd challenged him—if he needed to erase the past, then that made *them* impossible. He'd been stupid to be so honest, and she'd quickly figured out there was no fixing what had gone wrong between them. There was just no point in tiptoeing around the ugly truth. Still he smiled before he opened the door, because the truth was he had good news to share.

Like Shelby had once described working in a busy NYC

restaurant, controlled chaos was exactly what he found. He stood back and picked up on their rhythm. Tonight was more hectic than usual, because the house was full. Great news for The Drumcliffe, maybe not so much for the staff. They got paid by the hour, not the plates served.

Fred, a Cajun man from Louisiana who'd been at the hotel almost as long as Rita had, noticed Conor, dashed by and handed him the night's menu. He checked it out, quickly deciding on a traditional meal: clam chowder and king crab legs with what Shelby called hot potato salad, which was made from red potatoes, red onions and herbs and tossed with mustard, olive oil and garlic dressing, according to the menu. His mouth was watering already. It wasn't quite corn-on-the-cob season, so he'd settle for one of her delicious fresh greens salads with whichever artsy vinaigrette she'd devised for the day. Yeah. Sounded great, and his stomach sang in excitement.

Fred popped up again, took his order and sped off. Conor went to a corner of the long cutting board table to sit, trying to stay out of everyone's way.

Finally, from across the room at the stove with several huge pots of what he assumed were steaming crab legs, Shelby raised her head and noticed him. She wiped her forehead with her arm and lifted her brows in greeting.

"Busy night," he called out.

"Cray cray! I'm not sure what's happened, but I *like* it! I just hope we don't run out of crab."

Well, he was sure why it was crazy tonight, and as soon as he had the chance he'd explain it to her.

Fred delivered not a cup, but a bowl of chowder, chock-full of clams, and a slice of fresh corn bread. Not ordinary corn bread, but Fred's signature bread, cheddar with jalapeños. One bite and he was already in heaven. As he happily went about eating his meal, he surreptitiously watched

Shelby working nonstop. She knew, without a doubt, how to organize and run a kitchen, and pride welled up inside for her. The hot potato salad turned out to be the perfect complement to the crab legs. Wow.

When he was almost done, Shelby stopped at his section of the chopping island and went to work on a couple bundles of scallions. Could a person really use a knife that fast? Something on her hand caught his eye. He squinted and looked closer. A silver ring. It looked familiar.

Risking the loss of a finger or two, he reached across the chopping block and grabbed her right wrist to make her stop. He pulled her hand closer so he could have a better look. The Claddagh ring! She was wearing the promise ring he'd given her over ten years ago.

"What's this?"

"You know exactly what it is," she said, as she yanked her knife-holding hand away.

A flood of feelings hit him, anger leading them. "Take it off. You're mocking me by wearing that."

"I am not." Defiance sparkled in her eyes. "Besides, it's mine."

"You know exactly what the significance of that ring is." He caught himself pointing like he did when he read the riot act to an arrestee, so he consciously stopped. "And you have no business wearing it."

"I can wear *my* ring whenever *I* want." She raised her voice. Even in the rackety kitchen, her tone stood out and people turned their heads. "Besides—" she tamped it down "—I don't see it that way." She laid the knife down and gave him her total attention. "I've figured something out since the last time we talked. I can't erase my past, and furthermore I don't want to. It's made me exactly who I am." She used her index finger to poke at her own chest, and he was grateful she'd put the knife down first.

He hadn't finished his meal, but thanks to their tense interchange, he'd lost his appetite.

"The difference between you and me—" she pointed at him and continued "—is I can choose to move on and try again." She stared him down, and he didn't dare look away. "If you ever want a shot at happiness, I suggest you do the same."

"Is that a challenge?" Lame, but it was all he had in the comeback department, because she'd nailed it, and he'd turned defensive.

"Absolutely." She went back to chopping scallions. Chopping them to death.

He drank the last of his water, trying to clear his head. His hand was curiously unsteady. She had the craziest ways of knocking him off his game. *Just move on.* It sounded so easy, yet it'd never occurred to him. Because he was stuck. Back there on *that* night.

Frustrated and trying to clear his head, he took a bite of crab leg meat, chomping on it, forgetting to taste it. Then he remembered.

Besides eating dinner, he'd come here on a mission, to tell Shelby about the rave review. Why it mattered that she heard it first from him didn't make sense anymore. She was already mad at him and tossing out challenges. But he blundered on.

"Now that I've pissed you off—" he licked drawn butter off his fingers "—I wanted to share some good news."

She stopped for one second, tossed him an as-if-I-care glance, then went back to concentrating on the scallions. Poor scallions. "Is that so?"

"I thought you should know that Felecia Worthington wrote a rave review about The Drumcliffe and your cooking. Congratulations, chef, you made the county paper."

She dropped the knife. "What? She's a food critic?"

He wiped his hand with the paper napkin, then took the snipped article out of his shirt pocket and handed it to her. "You should be very proud," he said. "It came out in today's paper and it's probably why there's a line waiting to get in tonight. Never happened before in all the years I've been around." Then he walked off, leaving her with her mouth open, scrambling to unfold and read the article.

By the time he got to his car, there were footsteps rushing up behind him. Being in law enforcement, he tensed and turned, preparing for a possible altercation. But it was Shelby, running, out of breath, her face red, her eyes angry.

"Why didn't you tell me she was a food critic?"

"Didn't want to stress you out or put any undue pressure on you. You were doing me a favor."

Her anger softened a tiny bit. "Seems like you were the one doing *me* a favor."

He shrugged. "Works both ways."

"But if I'd known, I would have done something completely different, something that would've showed her who I am and what I can really do."

"You did that without knowing. Besides, from what I've learned, food critics never announce when they're showing up."

She folded her arms, obviously frustrated. "That's beside the point."

"That's the whole point. Damn, Shelby, do we have to argue about everything? Can't you just be happy about your great review?"

She closed her eyes briefly. "I'm sorry. I am happy, and excited, and...well, frustrated."

"Frustrated, why?"

"Because of you, Conor. Geez, don't you get it? I'm

asking you to give us another chance, and you set me up with a secret food critic who can launch my career."

"Just trying to help."

"Well, it ticks me off that you kept it a secret."

"So forgive me. It was to your advantage."

"Okay!" she yelled like she was still arguing instead of giving in. She calmed down and glanced at her chef clogs before seeking out his face again. "I forgive you, so let me take you on a date as a thank-you."

Her voice nearly inaudible.

He went quiet. Studied her, the woman who could rile him up faster than anyone else in the world. The woman who'd disregarded him at a key moment, and now expected him to simply move on. Go on a date! When everything was different now. "Let me think about it?"

"Is that your answer for everything?" A rhetorical question. He couldn't describe her expression, but it landed somewhere between angry, frustrated and willing. With a little disappointment thrown in. He'd have to settle for the willing part. "Look, I've got to get back to the kitchen. Like you said, it's standing room only tonight." And off she trotted.

The delicious meal he'd just eaten wrestled in his stomach. He hoped he hadn't thrown her off her game, not with the big crowd to feed. She'd worn the ring, sending a clear message, and it'd made him crazy. Why couldn't things be like they used to?

Because they were both nearly thirty now.

Time to act like a man? "I'll take you up on that date," Conor called, just before she hit the kitchen door.

"Cool, but it'll have to be a day date." She glanced toward the kitchen door as an explanation. "How about tomorrow morning at ten?"

She certainly didn't waste any time. So he gave the thumbs-up sign to the woman who'd hurt him like no one else. Ever.

Shelby tossed and turned in bed that night. She should be exhausted from running nonstop to serve nearly two hundred meals! A new record for her. Yet she couldn't go to sleep. Excitement, anger, frustration, happiness all rolled together in a barbwire tangle in her chest. What a mess she was.

She'd humbled herself and asked Conor flat out to give her another chance. Even asked him on a date. His hesitation didn't help a girl's ego much, but she could understand his point. Yet after the kisses they'd shared lately, she was positive they still had that special thing. Didn't he feel it, too?

Of course, starting a relationship over again took a lot more than turning each other on, but it sure was a great start.

In all fairness, she carried the most baggage. She had a baby now. He was still free as a sandpiper. Would a guy without a care in the world want to saddle himself with a kid, someone else's kid at that? Not to mention a woman who'd hurt him to the marrow? Who, as of last week, still had plans to find a bigger and better job and to kiss Sandpiper goodbye for good. Though now she wasn't so sure about that part.

Was his heart, the one she'd always known to be loving and generous, big enough to forgive her? Big enough for two? At least he'd said he'd think about it.

She'd asked for a day date for a reason.

If Conor spent more time around Benjamin, he'd have to see what a great kid he was. He'd already admitted he liked "Benny" as he'd called her son. So, yeah, that was what she needed to do, maybe not cram the Claddagh ring down his throat, stop wearing it for now, find another angle to get through to him, like making sure her two favorite guys had more time together.

First chance she got, she texted Conor to meet her and Benjamin at the park early Sunday morning. Recently, she and Fred had started alternating Sunday brunch service, and she was off. She might have to take baby steps where she and Conor were concerned, but she knew for a fact her Benjamin had the cutest toddler feet in the world, and even Conor would have to admit it. Where *she* might fall flat at winning her guy over again, her *boy* was sure to steal his heart.

Was she playing dirty? You bet.

Shelby showed up for the date armed. She'd brought a picnic basket filled with deli-styled sandwiches, macaroni salad, canned iced tea and cupcakes, Conor's favorite—spice cake with cream cheese frosting—a blanket to sit on, and toys for Benjamin, in case he got bored with the playground slides and swings. In typical toddler fashion, Benjamin wandered-walked somewhere in the vicinity around her as she headed into the park.

Conor was already there, sitting on the bench of a picnic table under a tree, which put a smile on her face. When he noticed her, he jumped to attention and strode to help carry all the stuff.

"Good morning," he said, looking chipper for a guy who worked late.

"Hi!"

Without being asked, he took the wicker basket and blanket. Upon noticing Conor, Benjamin sped up and headed in a straight line to catch up.

Conor bent down. "Hey, buddy, how's it goin'?" Her son stood silent. In awe?

"Say hi," she encouraged. He waved, which made Conor laugh, and once he put the basket on the table, he grabbed Benjamin and swung him around in greeting. Her son squealed in delight.

"Want to swing?" Conor asked him.

Benjamin pointed and shouted, "Fwing!"

"Swing?"

Off they went. Shelby smiled to herself over Conor's natural slide into helping Benjamin learn his words, then she stood and watched the big man and small boy interact at the swing set. A warm sensation filled her chest, along with an unexplainable yearning. Was this what she wanted? A father for her boy? What about the big city restaurant plans? Taking the culinary world by storm?

She remembered this was supposed to be a date, so instead of watching the "boys" and letting the sight dig deep and really get to her, she set up the picnic table with the cloth she'd brought. Then put the tiny plastic bud vase, with one perfect yellow rose from her mother's garden, at the center. After, she headed for the playground, where they'd now migrated to the slides.

"One, two, three," Conor counted before gesturing for Benjamin, who sat at the top, to let go and slide down. He started again. "One, two."

"Two, two," Benjamin repeated, then slid.

Shelby laughed. "Don't think he's mastered the counting concept yet." Then she made it to the bottom of the slide in time to catch her son before he did a face-plant in the sand. "He's a little slow on figuring out the ending part, too."

Conor chuckled. "Well, we're going to have to work on that, right, Benny boy?"

There went that yearning sensation again, and that pesky heart swelling. This date was either the best idea in the world, or a huge mistake.

After fifteen minutes or so on the slides, Conor helped Benjamin navigate the steps up the other equipment and, from the ground, assisted him across the bouncy rope and plank bridge. Which Benjamin found so fun, he repeated back and forth about six times, falling at least once every time. But it didn't stop him!

Conor passed Shelby what could only be described as proud grins, and her heart opened so wide she needed to sit, so she grabbed the nearest swing. *Let go, enjoy yourself. Right now feels like it always was with him.* Free. Fun. Sweet.

When Benjamin had finally had enough, Conor brought him to Shelby and put him in the kids' swing again. He stepped behind them and took turns pushing, first Ben, then Shelby. Her boy squealed with excitement as Conor pushed both of them higher and higher. And finally, she let go, let her heart soar as she pumped with her feet. Then, pulling a trick from her past, she launched from the swing, flying briefly and landing, not on her feet as she used to, but smack on her butt.

"Are you all right?" Conor asked, rushing to help her stand. She laughed and when he knew she was fine he joined her.

"I'm not as nimble as I used to be."

"Mommy fly."

"He's easily impressed," she said, rubbing her backside and dusting off sand, and enjoying the grin on Conor's face.

After Conor retrieved Benjamin from the swing, they went back to the picnic table to eat. From the basket, she doled out the sandwiches, and a special one for Benjamin.

She stood to do it, leaning forward to reach inside, then pass the food. After Conor set up Benjamin in a portable hook-on booster chair at the table, he stood beside her, his hand resting on her lower back.

"You sit down. I'll get the rest," he said. Such a gentleman.

It stopped her, the offer, yes, but mostly his touch. Was she playing with fire spending more time with him? What about her hopes and plans? Her profession? As she sat and let him finish serving, placing the bowl of macaroni salad in the center and removing the lid, in a tiny panic, she glanced around the park. Sandpiper was a small town— a person would never get famous here.

Wasn't that what she'd wanted all her life, to be noticed for her talent?

"You okay?" He asked as he sat beside her, obviously noticing her pushed-down brows and tense eyes.

"Oh, I'm good." She squeezed his thigh to reassure him, but all it did was make her want to drop her fork and kiss him. God, the man was solid. Could a girl be more confused? What was it going to be, stay or go? Would he ever consider coming with her?

Benjamin clapped at the sight of macaroni salad and she shifted gears from bargaining over her future, into mommy mode.

Later, after they'd annihilated the sandwiches, she brought out the cupcakes, and his knowing smile drilled straight through her heart. Yes, they were his favorite. Then, to show his appreciation, he kissed her, and she nearly forgot where she was. For that instant, all she knew was Conor, his spicy aftershave, tender lips and scratchy, in a good way, chin. And maybe the warm sun on her back.

She sighed, taking it all in, kissing him like it meant forever.

Until his beeper went off. He glanced at the number.

Before he dug out his phone from one of his cargo pant pockets, he put half a cupcake in his mouth and nearly downed it whole. He dialed, grinning with full cheeks and cream cheese showing. Benjamin thought it was hysterical, then fussed to get his own *cay-cay*.

Once Conor made contact, after she'd handed him a napkin, he listened intently while she helped Benjamin eat a bite of the cake part.

"I see. Okay. Be right there." He clicked off. "Sorry, gonna have to cut this picnic short. They need all units. More trouble out at the men's colony." His brows pinched as he considered what that meant, and her heart palpitated over the same thing. His job could be dangerous.

Their goodbyes may have been rushed, but without words, she let him know, as soon as possible, they'd pick up where they left off.

Before he left, he kissed her quickly again, then did the same to Benjamin, but on the crown of his head.

"Be careful!" she called out.

When he walked off, Benjamin cried.

Chapter Eight

Sunday night at The Drumcliffe Restaurant there was a lull in the dinner crowd just before 7 p.m. They stayed open until eight on Sundays and Shelby suspected only a few more stragglers might pop in. Conor had been on her mind all afternoon as she prepared for dinner. She left the kitchen in Fred's competent hands, and took the opportunity to sneak over to Padraig's Pub. There were very few certainties in the world, but the Sunday night Delaney family dinner was always a sure shot. The number of attendees might shift and change, but some assortment of family was always present and accounted for in the pub on a Sunday night.

Maybe if she played her cards right, she could become a regular again. That was a surprising component of her new hope anyway, and the plan was to not let Conor's resistance stop her.

Clearing her thoughts, she wandered from the restaurant, across the hotel lobby and registration desk, to the pub. As always on Sunday nights, the pub posted a sign—*Closed for private party.*

Opening the door, she peeked inside, expecting to see Conor and hear loud and friendly conversation as the Delaneys shared their meal around the long table back in the corner of the pub. Instead, no one was eating, and conversation was hushed. Everyone sat facing one of the large-screen TVs. Watching the news. She quickly realized Conor wasn't there, and come to think about it, she hadn't seen his patrol car parked out front, either.

Instead of interrupting them, Shelby stood right where she was and zeroed in on the story that captured everyone's attention.

"To repeat the top-of-the-hour news." The mature female newsperson continued, a tense expression on her face. "An ongoing protest at the men's colony in San Luis Obispo County has escalated to violence and riots. What had started as a peaceful protest in the minimum-security section of the west wing a couple weeks ago—a protest over decreased visiting hours and growing overcrowding—has spread to the east wing, where armed guards have lost control of the moderate security buildings. And where a dozen mental health workers are being held hostage."

Shelby caught her breath, her pulse doubling. That was what he'd been called in for, but she'd never imagined it could be this dangerous. So naive.

"All county sheriff departments have been called in to help control the heated protests on the minimum-security side, to allow increased manpower for the full-out riots and violence, plus the hostage situation, in the higher security building. We'll go live to the scene now."

Shelby stood clenching her hands, dread trickling through her, tension tying her tight, her mouth agape at what she witnessed on the TV. "Is Conor all right? Is he there?" Her voice was strained.

Maureen turned, alarm written over her face. Sean also turned. "He's been there all day."

How had she managed not to hear about this? She needed to sit down, but leaned on a nearby table instead. She'd been oblivious, only focusing on herself and Benjamin and her job. He'd acted so blasé about getting the call to go in early, probably not to worry her. "Have you heard from him?"

"Not since he said he was being sent with the riot units."

Riot units? Her heart hurdled through her chest, the pulse pounding in her ears. Maureen motioned for Shelby to come and sit with them. It took a moment to regain control over her legs to get there, but she settled next to Maureen.

The live action camera got bumped around, losing the shot. In the background, there were blurs of bodies tumbling and running, yelling and screaming. Then the camera straightened out again and there were law enforcement officers in full-out riot gear, pushing forward with riot shields, attempting to regain some semblance of control. In the background, more fighting and yelling, and total chaos.

"Word has spread through social media and there are now local protesters assembling outside the facility as well," the reporter continued. "Police are using tear gas, pepper spray and rubber bullets on the inmates." The TV footage showed police wearing helmets and body armor. They panned to the gathering protesters outside the facility. There the protests were escalating with some becoming violent, throwing homemade Molotov cocktails.

Where was Conor? Inside? Out? There wasn't a safe place for anyone, on either side. A few brave on-scene reporters attempted to give eyewitness accounts of what was going on, by getting as close to the fences as possible. Nearby protestors pushed around and roughed up some of them.

She could hardly manage to swallow. Maureen rubbed Shelby's forearm, mindlessly, as if to soothe herself. Shelby held Maureen's hand tight. Padraig paced and muttered. Daniel and Mark stood together, arms folded, watching every movement on the TV, making an occasional comment or curse. Laurel and Keela sat with arms around each other, completely quiet, the new baby swaddled and asleep on Keela's shoulder. The little girls weren't there, and Shelby figured Peter had been given babysitter duty and sent home.

Shelby decided to stay the rest of the night with Conor's family, preferring not to be worried out of her mind, alone. Here, watching the local TV coverage together with them helped keep her from falling apart. And drove the point home how much she cared for Conor. Hours later, when some progress had been made with crowd control, but not without multiple injuries, Padraig said, "I've seen enough. I know Conor's safe. I feel it here." He pressed a palm to his chest. "'Twont do us any good gawkin' at the TV screen till the wee hours."

With mild protest from Mark, he turned it off. Everyone sat quietly staring at each other, the air thickened by their unrelieved tension.

"What will be will be," Sean said quietly. "It's not like we can help."

"I'd like to know what's happening to my son," Maureen said, her jaw set and eyes tense with concern.

"We won't find out watching the news," Sean said. "It'll just make us sick with worry."

"Too late," she said.

Slowly things broke up, but Maureen still wasn't ready to let go of Shelby's hand. They gazed at each other, anxiety and fear making Maureen's normally bright green eyes dark and sad. Shelby's vision blurred for the umpteenth time, and they hugged. Again.

"I'll take you home," Daniel said. "Come with us." He guided Shelby from Maureen's grasp, out of the pub, to his car, then after first helping Keela and the baby get in the back seat, he helped Shelby into the front passenger seat. Due to the late hour, they'd agreed that Anna would sleep over at Laurel's.

In a daze Shelby made it home, completely unaware of the drive over. Her thoughts had gone inside, deep inside, where Conor was kept close to her heart. Once in her house, she checked on her son, then filled her mother in on the latest news, which wasn't necessary since Mom had been watching the Sunday night news earlier. Her mother hugged her and she went numb. Her only defense. When she fell into bed, she shuddered with fear, and stared at the ceiling the rest of the night, occasionally turning on her radio for an update. At 3 a.m. the riots still weren't completely under control.

Oh, God. How would she make it through the night? How would Conor?

The riots continued well into the next day, until the local unit of the National Guard was called in to assist, and the inmates were completely overpowered. It had been two days since Shelby had last seen Conor.

Early Tuesday morning Maureen called to inform her that Conor was back at the sheriff's department, where all the men were going through debriefing and getting interviewed by specially trained officers. Shelby's Monday off had been spent in worry hell, fighting to keep Benjamin from suspecting how upset Mommy was. She was thankful for the distraction of daily routine with her son. Otherwise she might have flipped out.

Maureen's news was such relief, Shelby finally could breathe, as if she'd been holding her breath for thirty-six hours.

When she got to work, the first thing she did was head to the registration desk. "He's okay?"

"He says he is," Maureen assured Shelby. She stepped around the counter and they hugged. Shelby had tried to keep herself occupied with Benjamin all morning. It had worked on Monday, but not very well today. After running around doing errands in town, it became time to get ready for work. She'd dropped Benjamin off at the elementary school office to wait the remaining few minutes before her mother was finished teaching for the day. The grandmotherly office clerk had grown to love her time with Benjamin the bashful. The thought made Shelby realize Benjamin had never been the least bit shy with Conor.

The radio news on at the registration desk filled both Maureen and Shelby in—though multiple injuries had occurred with the riots, fortunately the hostages had all been freed and there hadn't been any loss of life. Inside or outside of the prison.

And now Conor was being debriefed. She shuddered to think what he'd been through.

Thankful for the distraction of getting her kitchen up and running for the night, she plowed on with her day. Just before they opened the restaurant for dinner, Sean made an appearance. "All law enforcement officers eat free tonight."

Shelby smiled when her staff applauded his decision.

Many officers from within and without the area took the restaurant up on the offer, along with many new regulars, and Shelby had kept hopping throughout the evening, until the last meal was served.

Preoccupied with cleaning up the kitchen, she put the finishing touches on her cooking station. After a quick bathroom break, she glanced out the back window and swore she saw Conor's car parked in his usual spot.

"I'm going!" she called over her shoulder to her staff, as she hit the back door running, sprinting across the lot to Conor's ground floor suite. She banged on the door, not caring if she woke him or not. Brian answered. Disappointment swallowed her whole.

"Is Conor here?" she asked, breathless.

"Yes." His midnight hair and freakishly blue eyes blocked her entrance until he realized what he was supposed to do. Not nearly as tall as Conor, Brian stepped aside and let her in, and she rushed to the only closed door in the suite. She'd never been in his room.

He opened it before she was close enough to knock, and without hesitating she launched herself at him. So wrapped up in ragged emotions she hadn't given it a single thought. Out of reflex, he caught her, and continued to hold her near.

"You're okay?" Her legs wrapped around his waist, her arms resting on his wide shoulders.

"I'm okay." He was solemn.

It didn't stop her from twining her arms around his neck and kissing the hell out of him from relief. He looked tired, but gorgeous as always. She hoped he wouldn't mind her total attention, because nothing was going to call her off him. If he asked her to leave, she'd go limping off and curl up in a cave, never to come out again. But he didn't. In fact, he welcomed her and her kisses, then walked backward a few steps until they fell onto his bed.

They rolled around kissing and grabbing each other,

both needing physical touch to erase the tension and stress of the last forty-eight hours. She pulled at his undershirt, only then noticing his questioning gaze. She glanced over her shoulder. At some point Brian must have left for the bar, but Shelby got up and closed the door anyway. Then locked it to make her point.

She rushed toward the bed to Conor, with his beautiful green-blue interrogating stare. "Are you sure, Shel?"

It was the first time he'd called her "Shel" since she'd been home.

"More than anything." Diving onto him, taking his mouth with voracious kisses, pressing her skin flush with his, all she wanted was him. All of him.

They managed to undress each other without breaking the kisses. She loved how he smelled when he was turned on. Her hands eagerly scanned every part of him. There was bruising on his arms and back, and he winced when her hands skimmed his ribs, but nothing stopped him from loving her. Still, she worried she'd hurt him, so she held back a little. Hadn't he worn body armor?

She sat on her heels and studied him under the dim bedside light. He was as magnificent as she always remembered, and she'd missed him so, so much. The ache of how much translated to need.

Dizzy with desire, and more excited than she'd been in years, she couldn't wait to be with him. Her hand traveled up his thigh. He was unmistakably ready for her.

"I haven't been with anyone since I got pregnant," she whispered after devouring his ear. For some crazy reason, she wanted him to know that.

And it must have been what he needed to hear, because he reached in his bedside drawer and pulled out a little foil packet, then pulled her hips to his an instant after he was covered. Gently opening her, he made the long, delicious slide inside. She may as well have been on a rollercoaster with as quickly as he pulled her to the top, kept her tee-tering on the edge, begging, gasping, fighting for control. But she lost it almost immediately, massively and fiercely, and so, so amazingly.

Her dreamy groans and gasps served to incite him more. Within seconds, he prodded her back over the brink, which made him grin deviously, an expression she remembered from countless times before. "Let's see how many more you got left," he whispered over her ear, his breathing rushed, his lips hungry.

Only he knew her like this, vulnerable, completely under his control. She gave him everything, and thought she might die from these stretching, straining moments of bliss. Minutes later, with low humming in his chest, his arms stiffened and his hips stopped, but soon he recovered their lover's rhythm, to perfection, until he moaned and was completely lost to the moment. To them.

After recovering, with their breathing slowed and their tangled bodies settled into euphoric relaxation, Conor started talking. "You know there's only one way to erase the past. Right?"

Shelby raised herself from his chest, making sure she'd heard him correctly.

He lifted his head to meet her unsure stare, his prior drowsy expression now alert.

"Padraig calls it a Mulligan," he continued. "All we have to do is have a do-over. Let's start fresh, like it's the beginning. Date again. See what happens."

"Start fresh?" Obviously the sex had drained his brain, or he'd had an epiphany during the riots?

"Yes. That awful day? It's gone. Never happened. All we have is now and from now on." Was this the same guy wearing a wall three-feet deep she'd been banging her head against going all philosophical on her?

"Start fresh?" She loved repeating the words.

A new look of interest overtook his face. She reached for his jaw, gently pulling him to her, leaving no doubt she liked what he'd preached. "You mean like this?"

Chapter Nine

It hadn't been the riots that'd opened Conor's eyes, but the talk with the therapist during the debriefing. She'd said, don't go back to your life as though nothing has changed, go back and make it better. Choose one thing, and make a positive change. No way could Shelby argue with his crazy plan, pulling a Mulligan. Not with his hips planted tight against hers, and her topaz-brown eyes delving straight to his soul, and especially not after they'd spent the rest of the amazing night making up for six lost years.

There was only so long he could hold on to a grudge and apparently, along with Shelby's persistence and the therapist's wise recommendation, two years, seven months and change was his limit. He'd missed her. God, he'd missed her. At one point, he would have sworn he couldn't go on without her…until he did. Barely. But he didn't have to miss her anymore because he was pulling up to the curb at her house on the following Monday morning, to spend their entire day off together. Kid and all.

He'd gotten extra days off after the prison riots, and he and Shelby had scheduled more than a few dates together. Today was another "day" date, which meant Benjamin would be coming along. He parked the car and got out, not forgetting the red wooden pull-string train he'd picked up at the toy store on his way over.

Theoretically, he should resent the boy for being a constant reminder of Shelby's betrayal, but that wasn't his style. And Benny was sweet and funny—a hard combination not to like.

He knocked on her front door. Remembering his grandfather and his favorite golfing trick—pulling a Mulligan. He mentally patted himself on the back for coming up with a genius idea to help him finally get it.

"Hi," she said, with a genuine smile, a spring to tippy toes and an expectation of a hello kiss. He didn't waste a second before giving her what she wanted. His reward— bright eyes and a sexy grin that all but said out loud, "I can't wait for Benjamin's afternoon nap."

Neither could he. She looked great, as usual, in crop-length olive green pants that hugged her hips tight, wedge sandals, which helped the tiniest bit with the huge height difference between them, and a formfitting brown tank top. Nothing about her was overdone, and he sure liked the way her measurements added up. More importantly, how she felt when he held her close.

"Bah-blo!" The kid wore khaki-colored shorts, a dark blue shirt with a tiny bear applique above a useless pocket, and mini versions of a popular sports shoe.

Conor had no clue what that *Bah-blo* meant, but Benny boy was heading in his direction with a stuffed something in one hand and half a banana in the other. "Hey, buddy." He dropped to a knee for the official greeting.

Benjamin must have thought that was funny, because he giggled up a storm, inadvertently crushing the tip off the banana, only then noticing with a bewildered glance as it fell to the floor.

Shelby rushed to Benjamin's aid, picking up the dropped fruit, wiping his hand and delivering some smooshed banana from his palm to his mouth. Undaunted, he made the last few steps to Conor, swatting his thigh when he reached him, which made Benjamin laugh all over again.

"I got something for you."

"Is it?" Benjamin said, looking everywhere except behind Conor's back.

He displayed the bag, then opened it for Benny to have a peek inside. "It's a train."

"Tay-no!"

"Train," Conor said slowly as the boy watched his mouth.

"Tay-no!" Benjamin grabbed and ran, holding the bright green engine, the attached-by-string blue boxcar and red caboose dangling behind. "Tay-no!"

"Let me show you how it works." Conor coaxed the pull train from the boy's death grip, set it on the floor and showed him how to pull the string as he walked around the small living room. Already, Conor had learned that asking Benny to walk was a joke, and the boy took off at his usual jog on his sturdy short legs, soon dragging the train on its side, instead of on the small wooden wheels from living room, to the dining alcove, to the kitchen and back. But he didn't care because he knew how to have fun.

Something Conor had nearly forgotten, until he'd started hanging with a toddler. And his mom, again.

He glanced up at Shelby, who had a strange look in her eyes. Not quite sad, more like wishful, and he almost understood why. Things had gotten all messed up between them over the years, and if he'd had his way, their history would have him in it, and maybe a kid like Benjamin in it, too. Which made him wonder what Shelby's version of wishful history might be. Maybe he could entice her to tell her version by using some of her favorite moves later, when they hit the sheets.

He understood the past couldn't be changed, but he was still curious. Probably always would be. "You ready for the park?"

"Absolutely. Just let me get the picnic basket."

"I'm going to get fat hanging out with you all the time." Benjamin was still running around dragging the new toy behind him, now extending the route to include the hallway.

"If memory serves me, we always manage to work off the calories," she said from the kitchen, giving him a great view of her backside.

Flashes of the many ways they'd been working off calories for the last week of April had him mentally undressing her.

"I beg your pardon," she said, teasingly, when she reentered the living room with picnic basket in hand, presumably reading his mind. "There's a young child in the room." She passed him a smoldering gaze that zipped up his leg and simmered below his belt. The day was looking up, and the afternoon promised to be unforgettable.

The first Tuesday morning in May, Conor had made an appointment with the realty agent he'd been dangling along over his intention to buy the Beacham House for the last year or so.

"I've mentioned before," the ready-to-retire, silver-haired and tanned gentleman started. "You don't have to have twenty percent down payment to bid on a house these days."

"I know, it's just there's a lot of building still to do and repairs that I'll need to take care of, too."

"I'm working on getting you the best price possible. Shall we go have a look at the current state of the place?"

Would it be any different than three months ago, the last time he'd gone for a house tour? Shelby and Benjamin popped into his mind. Yes. Because lately his future looked bright, and a man with a bright future needed a house…to share all that future-ness.

Shelby came to work a half hour early Thursday afternoon to meet Mark. The kitchen smelled like last night's root vegetables side dish, and caramelized onions, so she left the back door open. The move had nothing to do with being able to keep an eye on Conor's car, or his hotel suite. Though she did keep peeking out back until Mark showed up.

Since she'd started the new job, they'd had brainstorming meetings every other week. Mark had grown a distinguished-looking beard that made his bright blue eyes stand out even more than usual. The Delaney men all had devastating eyes, easy to get lost in. Shelby was sure of one thing: Conor's were the only eyes she wanted to float away in, and it had been that way since their very first kiss.

"I've got some great news," Mark said, opening his notebook-styled computer, setting it on the center island and booting it up. "We have steadily increased business in the two months you've been here."

Shelby could have told him that, as a plate counter

from back in NYC, but seeing the graph made her grin. "Terrific."

"Indeed. In fact, the hotel business has picked up, too, and May is usually a slow-down month before summer starts." He shared a victorious grin, and Shelby understood why Laurel had fallen for him. "So, I wanted to throw out some suggestions, but first I'd like to hear anything you'd like to try."

At any given time, Shelby had ten different ideas zipping around her mind for how to improve business. Today, she planned to share two of them. "I'm glad you brought up the uptick in hotel bookings, because I've been thinking of adding a theme night during the week. Say, on Thursday nights, when we are slower than the weekend. We could offer some sort of package deal for our guests, you know something like, add Thursday night to your weekend stay and enjoy a special themed meal from our chef." She scratched her nose, wishing her idea had come out better. It'd seemed great in her mind, but saying it out loud suddenly made her insecure. "For instance, how about a *Titanic* night, where everything I serve would be something that had been served on the *Titanic*. Or a Roaring Twenties night, where guests will experience a typical menu from that era, or how about a night-in-Paris dinner. Oh, and to start off the holidays, we could have a Victorian Christmas theme in early December. You know, that kind of thing."

Mark's gorgeous eyes brightened. "I think those are all great ideas. It might also appeal to people in the area looking for something different to do. Especially after summer and during the holidays."

"Yes, of course, but to bring in more hotel guests, they should get first dibs on booking, and because some of the meals might be extravagant, I'd need to limit how many to serve."

"You mean, like only one sitting for the night?"

"Or two, depending on how many people want to partake."

"Maybe at first, you know just to see how things go, we could reserve the main lobby area and make this a themed happy hour, appetizer kind of thing?"

He was pulling back a bit, but his enthusiasm level hadn't changed. She could compromise, and it made sense to try something out on a smaller scale, rather than go for broke right off. Her motto in New York used to be "no risk, no gain," but sometimes small steps made more sense. Plus, she had the Delaney family to answer to if her great idea wound up tanking.

"Do you trust me to go with this, Mark? I'll do my best not to let you down."

"I think it's a great idea." His confidence in her was obvious. "Let me run it by my parents—" That statement threw her: What happened to believing in her all the way? But something clicked behind his eyes the instant he mentioned his parents. His chin jutted out the slightest bit, and resolution set his mouth in a straight line. "No, you know what, I'm making an executive decision on this. Let's do it. When do you want to start?"

Wow, she hadn't expected such cooperation from her boss, and it excited her. "Uh, well, we need some time to get the word out, social media and all that, so how about two weeks? Let's try the *Titanic* night first. I'll work up a menu and get it to you ASAP so you can post it on the website."

"Excellent, and I can print up flyers for local businesses to hand out, oh, and I'll do a mailer to past guests."

"Yes, all great ideas, bring them back. If the guests like the idea, you could get monthly bookings!"

Mark grinned, rubbed his beard with one hand and put his other hand on her shoulder, patting her back.

"This idea of yours could put The Drumcliffe on the map."

"You think?"

His expression changed from excited to curious. "You really don't get how talented you are, do you."

"Well, I was beginning to hold my own with a few of the chefs back in New York, but..." Along came Laurent.

"And Paris. Didn't you study there for a while?"

"Uh, yes." Her heart started to sink, her shoulders got heavy, remembering Laurent. He may have been the dumbest move in her life, but aside from getting blind-sided by his charm, she'd learned amazing things in his kitchen. And he'd inadvertently given her the greatest joy of her life in Benjamin. Now, at the humble Drumcliffe Hotel, she'd finally get a chance to show her stuff.

"I don't want you to ever feel trapped in a dead-end job, Shelby. Always feel free to share your ideas with me."

"Thank you. And on that note, didn't you say you had some ideas, too?"

"Yeah, but nothing like yours. Well, sort of like yours except I was going with the appetizer and cocktails kind of thing." Which was exactly what they'd landed on by the end of their conversation. Shelby may just be an ob-server, but Mark showed great talent in running the hotel. And being honest, she liked his roll-out idea of appetiz-ers and drinks better than her totally disruptive themed-menu idea. "Let's do this," he said. "Let's get your name on the Central Coast map for great chefs."

"I'll do my best, boss." Was it possible for a heart to

sing, because she was pretty sure that was what hers was doing.

They looked at each other, totally friends, in complete respect of each other's business sense, then shook hands on the deal.

"I'll expect to see that menu mock-up by tomorrow," Mark said as he left the kitchen.

Wow, sooner than she'd thought. With added urgency, she put the ideas otherwise floating around in her head to paper. If this had happened while she was in New York, she'd be on a list of chefs to watch! But opportunity knocked in the strangest places, and this time it happened in Sandpiper Beach. Time to get serious about knocking more socks off.

Then she took another glance out the back door to Conor's hotel suite. He was probably still sleeping from working the night shift, and the idea of knocking some socks off, in a whole different setting, really took hold.

"Taste this." Shelby followed Conor around her small family kitchen with a spoonful of sabayon sauce while he cleared dinner plates and put them in the sink to rinse and load in the dishwasher. He complied, tasted the sauce, then made that heavenly expression she loved.

"What's in it?" He stopped loading his arm with plates long enough to ask.

"Egg yolks, champagne, tarragon, butter." She'd gone back to stirring the saucepan.

"Kill me softly, Shel," he whispered over her shoulder, sending an unintended message to her nether parts.

"I know." She laughed, covering for her straight-to-sex reaction. "If it tastes delicious, it's bad for us." She hoped that didn't transfer to relationships. As in theirs.

They'd had a simple dinner at her house since her

mother had an overnight meeting down in Ventura. Fortunately, Conor was scheduled off work, too. Now they played "family" even to the point of Benjamin insisting Conor put him to bed. That move had allowed Shelby to test her sauce recipe.

What amazed Shelby was how willing Conor had been to play along. Hope welled up inside. Could he be willing to accept both of them? Hold on, she chastened herself, the guy hit the ceiling when she'd worn his Claddagh ring. Though he'd signed on to the starting fresh idea, he hadn't come close to whispering *I love you* after sex, either—of which there had been plenty of opportunities in the last couple weeks. At least he'd started calling her "Shel" again, a nickname she had never been particularly fond of until now, when it mattered so much.

They'd had a fun dinner. Benjamin loved eating hamburger meat and colorful vegetables, and come to think of it, so did Conor. Especially since he'd grilled the burgers out back. Her only contribution on her Monday night off was to bake homemade sweet potato fries. Benjamin loved those, too. As did Conor. Men were so easy to please.

"What's the sauce for?" He got back to the business of rinsing and loading.

"I'm putting nice plump seared scallops in this sauce as part of the *Titanic*-themed appetizers."

"Great idea you and Mark came up with, by the way."

"Your brother is amazing. He makes me feel like I'm the best chef on earth, and that only makes me want to prove him right."

Conor faced her. "You know he resisted taking over the hotel, like it was the last thing in the world he'd ever want to do."

"Seriously? He's so good at it."

"He is, isn't he." Pride was the only way to describe Conor's expression.

He turned back to the sink and dishwasher duty, so she put down her stirring spoon and went up behind him, then hugged his torso, placing her cheek against his back, loving his warmth and strength, never wanting to let go. "You know what he said to me?"

"Hmm." His hum rumbled against her face.

"He didn't want me to ever feel trapped in his kitchen, so he'd always welcome any ideas I had."

Conor went still, but only for an instant so as not to alert Shelby to his reaction. Mark had taken their conversation about Mom and Shelby to heart. Obviously, Mark agreed with Conor, so he'd started this new themed happy hour bit, to challenge Shelby and keep her from getting restless.

He still worried it would only be a matter of time before Shelby got restless again.

"He also came up with the ingenious idea of showing your mother's paintings in the lobby on easels every Sunday afternoon. That's the mark of a successful businessman—innovation. Don't you think?"

He turned to face her. "Absolutely." This too had been the result of Conor's concerns for Shelby based on his gut feelings about his mother and her art. "Mom should get a kick out of that."

The thought of his mother having regular showings of her oil paintings made Conor happy. Even though the gesture might be too little too late. He forced a smile.

Shelby always liked it when he smiled. In fact, this time, she seemed to like it so much, she gave that "come get me" look, the one he loved seeing above all others.

"You know what I'd really get a kick out of?" she said, moving closer, placing her hands on his shoulders.

"Hmm?" He leaned against the counter, trying to act cool.

"Forgetting about the dishes and heading straight to my room." One thinly arched brow shot up with the suggestion. Her hands started a slow slide from his shoulders over his chest, and down his ribs leaving tingly paths the entire way. "I want to be the one doing the tasting this time…" From beneath her thick lashes she gave a seductive glance. "…of you."

She may as well have shot a lightning bolt through him.

An hour later, after a whole lot of tasting and taking turns had been going on, Conor pulled Shelby to his chest. She hoped tonight might be the night he told her he loved her again. The one and only time they'd said it to each other was on the beach six years ago. She still remembered the sound of his voice and her breathless reply. *I love you.* Then they'd made a promise. The very promise she'd blown two plus years back. Maybe she should take the lead this time? But what if it fell flat?

"You know what I think," he said, mindlessly rubbing her lower back.

That you love me? "Nope." She played with a button on his shirt, giving him time to broach the subject.

"We should take a shower."

Boing went the sound of her hopefulness as it hit the ground and bounced away. Foolhardy as it may be, she was determined to lay it out there for him tonight. She'd put everything else out there these last few weeks, and he'd willingly taken part…every chance they had. "A shower sounds great, but not before I tell you something." She lifted her head and found his questioning eyes. Her lips pressed together, then she went for it. "I'm in love with you." First chills circled her skin, followed by the heat of doubt.

"Shel," he said, wrapping his fingers at the back of her

head and drawing her near. "I've pushed so much down for so long, those words don't come easily to me anymore."

"You mean you didn't mean them before?"

"No, I did. I meant them." He hugged her close, as if willing her to understand, then talked over her scalp. "I'm not trying to beat a dead subject, but you hurt me."

"I've changed."

"I know we're starting fresh, but in the back of my mind, I keep wondering how long before you'll feel trapped here, and want to move on."

"Everything is different now," she said, both feeling and sounding defensive.

"I've gotta take this slowly."

She broke from his hold to make eye contact again. "Well, we sure aren't taking sex slowly."

"You started it." His chin looked like Mark's had when he'd made that snap decision.

"I know." She couldn't deny the truth, if Conor wasn't ready.

"You can't force me to be on your timeline. I'm not the guy you used to know."

"I know that, too." Hell, she'd helped make him the skittish-about-love kind of man he'd turned into. All the great feelings she'd just shared with him, and the hope she'd built up for when they could be together as a couple again, evaporated like morning beach fog.

Conor was afraid of loving her. She'd made him that way, and knowing it cut through her heart like a butcher knife. Mulligan or not, he was still remembering the pain she'd inflicted on him. Could she blame him?

He gently removed her from his chest, got out of bed, then laced his fingers through hers and drew her to her feet. He tugged her along to the bathroom, for that shower he'd suggested, and she dutifully followed.

If this was all he could offer, she'd take it, because the thought of going back to life without him was completely unacceptable.

Chapter Ten

Monday morning they met up for another hike. Shelby suggested it would be a good thing to get his mind off the prison riots. Who was he to disagree, since other than the moments he spent making love with Shelby or arguing about taking things fast or slow, the prison riot was the only thing he'd thought about.

This time they drove north to the Point Lobos loop trail. Much of it paralleled the ocean in Carmel by the Sea, with breathtaking views. Benjamin had napped for the drive, and was now wide-awake and anxious to move. Halfway into the trail, it occurred to Conor how he'd gotten good at hiking with a kid in a back carrier, hardly noticing the extra weight. Enjoyed it even.

"Hey, look." He pointed out to sea. While waves crashed around a rocky finger of land, loud barking overpowered the sound of the ocean. "Look at all the sea lions."

"Wow. Benjamin, see the sea lions? They're sunbathing on the rocks."

Benjamin saw some movement, clapped his hands and kicked his feet.

Seeing him happy made Conor happy.

Further down the path they found a perfect spot to picnic. As always, Shelby had come prepared with sandwiches, drinks and fruit. They sat in a grassy area where wild yellow mustard flowers bloomed, enjoying the meal.

Benjamin was happy to get out of his carrier and run around chasing butterflies. When he started chasing bees, Shelby stepped in. "Come back over here, I have a treat for you."

When it came to being a mom, Shelby was a natural, and it never ceased to impress Conor.

From the well-manicured trail, they went off the path and carefully hiked over slippery rocks to get to the tide pools. Just before they reached their destination, Shelby's boot slipped and she shrieked. Before she hit the rocks, Conor lunged and caught her, nearly losing ground in the process. They struggled to regain their balance but prevailed.

"Thanks!" she said, winded. "That would've hurt."

Feeling alarmed and protective, he didn't let go right away, but spent the time looking into her eyes. Her pupils were widened from the near fall. Out of fear for her being hurt, his were probably dilated, too. He never wanted Shelby to get hurt.

Her cheeks were flushed and the sea breeze whipped her hair around. The vision was too inviting. Moved by a surge of emotion, he kissed her while she leaned back in his embrace, the way he'd caught her. Midkiss, it occurred to him, at this crazy angle, they might compete for that iconic 1940s kissing pose between a sailor and a nurse, but in his opinion, the Pacific Ocean was a much better backdrop than NYC.

"Blahk blahk." Not nearly as caught up in the moment as Conor and Shelby, Benjamin kicked Conor's kidneys and pointed to a group of pelicans high in the sky, diving head first into the sea.

After he helped Shelby to full standing position, they all watched the unique fishing technique of the pelicans, and today Conor related to it. When you want and need something, go for it. Dive in!

Wasn't that the point of starting fresh?

After a week of no-questions-asked sex, Conor showed up in The Drumcliffe kitchen with a wide smile displaying nearly every single one of his gorgeous teeth.

"You look like a man who just found a million dollars," Shelby said, whipping together the ingredients for the night's special seafood soufflé. Every week the dinner crowd grew, and the signups for the *Titanic*-themed appetizer gathering were already full. Come to think of it, Shelby had a lot to smile about, too, but right now the man with the proud grin was her reason.

"Better than that." Hands on his hips, board shorts, name-brand T-shirt, looking like a beach bum god, what could be better?

"Wow, a billion?" She whipped faster.

"FTO."

She pulled in her chin, not having a clue. "Did you just cuss at me, or is that some kind of money?"

"Field Training Officer." He gave her a deadpan stare, nearly drilling through her heart. "I'm getting a promotion."

She stopped whipping and put the stainless-steel bowl on the counter, wiping her hands on her apron-covered hips. "Fantastic! Is it because we wined and dined your boss?"

"I hope not. Didn't mean to bribe him with your cooking." He leaned on one elbow on the counter, kind of like hanging out at the pub. "I think it has more to do with the riots and my stellar conduct under extenuating circumstances, to quote Captain Worthington's 'indication for the job' endorsement."

"Wow de-dow! This is great. Congratulations." Her instinct was to hug him, but being at work held her back.

"Definitely worth a celebration."

"Am I invited?"

"You're the first person I thought of." Now she really wanted to hug him.

"Before your parents?"

"That'll come later. First I have a different kind of celebration in mind."

"Oh, *that* kind—"

"—of *celebration*. Yeah."

They'd been spending so much time together they'd fallen back into finishing each other's sentences, which Shelby loved. She wondered if Conor was even aware of it. "So what do you have in mind?" She batted her lashes, hinting at all the fun they could have on the box springs.

"A date. A *hot* date. Where I take *you* out for dinner for a change." He fiddled with the sleeve of her dusty rose chef jacket, nearly making the matching toque spin on her head. "Of course, it'll be hard to find a place on the same scale with your talent."

"Oh, you flatter me."

With that he stood, stepped closer and sent her the sincerest look a guy six foot three could give a pipsqueak like her without seeming to look down his nose. "We'll have to drive all the way to Carmel again."

"Not…" She'd been telling Conor about an Italian restaurant with amazing write-ups that she'd wanted to scout out sometime on her day off.

"La Balena. Yes."

Her hands came to her mouth, and it took everything she had not to jump up and down like Benjamin did when he was excited.

"You happy?"

"More than you know. This sounds more like *my night* than celebrating your promotion."

"I'll be sharing it with you, for all the good things we've both accomplished."

His intentions seemed too meaningful, especially for a guy gun-shy on opening his heart again. "The difference is, I didn't have to get in the middle of a riot to get here."

"No, but you had to come home and face me." There went his earnest look, complete with tented brows. "That had to be tough."

She tugged on the hem of his untucked T-shirt, swearing this moment had something to do with making progress on the sea of mistakes between them. "Well worth the fight, in case you hadn't noticed."

He slipped his hand around her waist and drew her closer, then, doing what she didn't have the guts to do in her own kitchen, bent to kiss her. After taking his time, using his mouth in ways she'd never grow tired of, he ended the kiss on his terms. As always, leaving her wanting more. "I'm glad you came home."

Now that was progress! Of course a gazillion questions started forming in her mind, but now wasn't the time. She especially wanted to ask if that meant she could start wearing the Claddagh ring again, but thought better of it, not wanting to spoil the cushy-sexy tone. Too bad she had a couple hundred meals to prepare for the night, because her body was thinking of ways to celebrate this special moment, right here and now.

"Sunday night. Have Fred deal with the dinner crowd. I'll pick you up at seven."

It was hard being a chef and trying to maintain a social life. At least in a small town like Sandpiper Beach, where she worked for her boyfriend's family, she could ask for a night off every once in a while. Conor's promotion was the perfect excuse, too. Even though Sunday night was always Delaney family dinner night, under the circumstances of his promotion, how could Mark refuse?

Sunday night, Conor wore his nicest slim-fit pale blue dress shirt and a pair of straight-legged navy trousers. He'd even thought about wearing a tie, but decided not to, though he did want to look his best for Shelby. He'd been thinking things through about the two of them, how long they'd known each other, how far they'd come in life and, after nearly a ten-year hiatus, how they still had feelings for each other. A whole lot of feelings. He couldn't deny what they had was special.

His promotion to Field Training Officer was not only a step up, but a raise. The Beacham House was becoming more and more within his reach. But he still had to deal with the surprising sting that sometimes cropped up when he was around Benjamin. The kid was cute, and fun, that wasn't the issue. It was surreal knowing Shelby had had a child with another man. Blunt though it may be, that was the truth. His truth. He wasn't proud of it, but nevertheless...

Having a family had always been part of his secret dreams...about Shelby. He'd never been able to see that bigger picture with Elena—because there hadn't been one—and she'd picked up on it. They'd broken up amicably enough, but he'd still seen it as a failure. All because of Shelby still having a hold on his heart.

He tapped on her front door and waited. She opened it in a fitted black sheath with a high jewel-type neck, but with cross straps showing lots of shoulder and back. He wondered how the dress might look turned around, though he wasn't complaining. She looked sexy. Her caramel-colored hair was parted on the side, as she always wore it, with the bangs playing peekaboo over one arched brow, and the blunt cut ends cupping just below her earlobes. It had taken a while, but he'd come to really like her with her new shorter, more sophisticated hairstyle. But what he liked the most right now was how the haircut drew full attention to those long, dangly turquoise bead earrings swaying with her every move. Mesmerizing. He saved the best for last, sweeping his gaze over her legs. He couldn't very well call them long, with her being all of five foot two, but they were finely shaped. Then on to the strappy shoes giving her a few gained inches on him and reveal-ing a scarlet pedicure. Sex personified.

Hard to believe, under the circumstances of where his thoughts had just sprinted, the best part of all was how the tense look in her eyes had disappeared since she'd first come to town. Over the course of the last couple months, as she had learned to relax, she'd also gained back some of her lost weight. Every day, she was more like the Shelby he used to know, but also the incredible person she'd be-come. "Wow. You look great."

She blushed, and after all the times they'd been to-gether lately, that simple act of her turning pink made a bigger impression than the little black dress and painted toes ever could.

"You look hot, too," she said, still recovering from her blush, and making his mind wander to how things would go after dinner, when it was just the two of them. He'd kicked Brian out of the suite for the night, and he had high hopes her mother would take over with Benjamin until the morning.

He couldn't deny his feelings any longer. Shelby, since her return, had managed to break open his heart again and force her way inside.

The day had finally come for the first ever Thursday night themed appetizer and cocktail party at The Drumcliffe Hotel lobby, held in the solarium alcove. Seventy-five guests had signed up, leaving only the remaining twenty-five slots for locals, which, when combined with the serving staff and hosts, would just about equal the 150-person occupancy allowed per the local fire department for that space.

After two months of running her own kitchen, she was nervous about that night and the new venture. The menu: cold asparagus truffle vinaigrette with soft quail egg, the seafood sabayon she'd tested on Conor, cod or lamb à la française, chocolate and vanilla fondant over crunchy honeycomb, and of course classic French cheese with Waldorf garnish, complemented with a champagne-and-orange sorbet punch, all for the totally reasonable price of admission. Padraig would handle the cash bar for any other drinks, and in fact, had assigned Brian to that detail.

Shelby woke up early Thursday morning thinking about the night ahead, and all the hours it would take to prepare for it, but she woke up for another reason, too. Benjamin was crying, and not in a "Good morning, I'm awake" kind of way. This was the distinct, piercing sound of a boy in pain.

She rushed out of bed to his room, finding him standing, his flushed face covered in tears. "Ma maaah!"

She picked him up and held him close, feeling a feverish head. Her heart quickened. What could be wrong? She checked the clock. By the time they both got dressed and drove to the urgent care clinic Conor had introduced her to when Benjamin had bronchitis, the place should be open.

The timing of his illness couldn't be worse, but she'd learned early on how, at any given moment, being a parent could annihilate all other plans. Her mother worked today as usual, and, of all nights, had an administration meeting at the elementary school.

Panic seeped into Shelby, taking over her bloodstream and driving up her pulse. She wouldn't be able to make the dishes for tonight if Benjamin was sick.

The nurse called them in, and soon enough, the diagnosis proved Shelby's hunch —an early ear infection. His inner ears were tight as drums with fluid. Even though the nurse administered liquid ibuprofen, Benjamin only minimally improved. All he wanted was to be held by Mommy, and there was no way she could run a kitchen with a twenty-five-pound toddler in her arms.

What would she do?

Without thinking, she took out her cell phone and called Conor to explain her situation. When she'd finished, she couldn't believe the words coming from his mouth. *I'll take care of him.*

Could she let go and leave her precious son with Conor while Benjamin was sick, so as not to ruin the big night?

If she didn't want to risk her reputation, let Mark and the Delaneys down, not to mention the 150 people expecting tonight to happen, she'd have to take Conor up on his offer.

Conor listened carefully as Shelby explained which medicine to give when and how much. Red liquid for pain and white liquid for fever, every four to six hours.

"That's it?"

"They don't hand out antibiotics like they used to for ear infections. We are in wait-and-see mode. If his temperature goes up, or if he seems in more pain…"

"I'll take him to his doctor."

"I was going to say, you can add the ibuprofen. Alternate the medicine. Also, prop his head up when he sleeps so the pressure won't build up behind his ears." She must have seen the growing concern in Conor's eyes, because she stopped in the middle of the instructions and patted his hand. "If you don't think you can do this—" Maureen, a woman with three kids under her belt, had also offered to watch Benjamin to free Shelby for the big event tonight once she'd heard about the problem, but Conor insisted on taking the job so his mother could join in with the fun.

"No. I'm going to take care of Benny boy here, right?" He looked at Shelby's son, who showed signs of being in less pain now than when he'd first arrived, so he crossed his eyes and made a funny face. For his effort, Benjamin gave a half laugh. Conor suspected it was more out of courtesy than for his skill at clowning around.

It took a lot of convincing, but she packed up during Benjamin's midmorning nap and left for the restaurant. When the house was totally quiet, Conor tiptoed into the boy's room to check on him. As he watched Benjamin deeply asleep, curled up around the small pillow Shelby had hoped would keep pressure from building in his ears, Conor got blindsided by a feeling: worry.

He rolled his shoulders, realizing how tense he'd been all morning, watching the kid suffer. It'd hurt him and made him wish he could take the pain instead of Benny, who clearly didn't deserve to feel that way.

Conor smiled over the crib, thinking the child seemed to be in some state of nirvana. As he stood there, another thought occurred to him, and it had something to do with the warm sensation circulating in his chest. He cared for the boy, and not just in an isn't-he-cute kind of way, but with real feelings that reached deep inside and tugged on all kinds of heartstrings in myriad different directions. So confusing. Was this a taste of how it felt to be a parent?

Shelby couldn't believe how well the *Titanic*-themed party was going. Then guilt struck like the iceberg that sank the ship. Her baby was home sick, how could she possibly enjoy herself? She'd been so busy with preparing and serving the food, she hadn't thought about him in, she glanced at her watch, at least an hour. Until today, her mother was the only other person in the world she relied on to care for her boy. Now there was Conor, whom she trusted on every level.

Early on, alone in New York City without options, she'd had to leave her baby with caregivers she really didn't know, and the thought of ever having to repeat those anxious times made her queasy. How had she done it, survived without support of family or close friends?

She shook her head, focused back on the loud party and admitted those days were over. Taking a deep breath, she glanced around the full-to-capacity room where people smiled, laughed, ate and drank while sharing lively conversations. A half-dozen women who were staying at the Prescott B&B came in turn-of-century Edwardian-era dresses with puffy sleeves, cinched waists and pointy shoes, complete with huge hats straight from the 1990s *Titanic* movie. As Shelby stood there, noticing that everyone appeared to be having a blast, even Sean and Maureen Delaney, Maureen approached her.

"How's Benjamin doing?" Conor's mother asked, pushing her face close so Shelby could hear.

How could she answer that she hadn't checked in lately, without sounding like a horrible parent? "I think okay. At least Conor hasn't sent any texts or called."

"Good. I was surprised he'd volunteered."

"You're not the only one."

"I think you're the only person on the planet he'd do it for."

Shelby had wondered the same thing, and hearing it come from Mrs. Delaney drove the point home. Conor's offering to take care of Benjamin was nothing short of heroic.

If their relationship kept on at this rate, she'd be ready to propose to him by summer. Who cared about tradition, he was the guy she wanted to spend the rest of her life with!

She felt a buzzing in the pocket of her chef's jacket, fished out her phone and saw a text from Conor. Her heart dipped with concern, until she read it.

All is well. Benjamin is eating a second bowl of cereal.

He'd attached a photo of her boy chowing down as proof.

She grinned, noting his hair looked damp, like maybe the fever had broken. A good thing. Then another picture came through, a selfie with the two of them smiling like they had a big secret, and Conor looking far too much like perfect daddy material.

She had to face the facts, he was a hero and a half, but did that make him too good to be true?

She shared the photo with Maureen. "Speaking of the little angel." Her chest swelled with relief for her son, and love for Conor's consideration. How did he know she was just wondering and worrying about Benjamin? And him, too.

"Aw, he's so adorable. Glad he's doing okay. And would you look at that, Conor's a natural." *In more ways than one.* With that, Maureen gave Shelby a hug and went off to mingle.

Shelby was just about to return to the kitchen to replenish the lamb and cod offerings when a distinguished-looking man in a gray suit approached.

"Chef Brookes?"

She stopped and offered her handshake. "Yes. Hello."

"I'm Damian Black."

She had a distinct memory of seeing the salt-and-pepper-haired, tanned gentleman in the restaurant before. A week or two ago? He'd stood out from the usual crowd in that he'd worn a sophisticated three-piece suit on that visit, too. Now her interest was piqued.

"Looks like your *Titanic* tasting event is a huge success. The appetizers are all delicious, I might add."

"Thank you."

"I first heard about The Drumcliffe Restaurant from a stellar write-up in the *Central Coast Ledger*, and decided to pop in to see if your talent was as good as Felecia Worthington insisted." He paused, and gave a relaxed, charming smile. "I'm happy to say I wasn't disappointed."

"I'm so glad. Thank you for telling me. We're trying to bring the restaurant to a new level and reach out to foodies in the tri-county."

"You've definitely raised the level of cuisine, and that's why I'm here tonight."

Her pulse quickened with curiosity. "Sir?"

"Shelby?" Fred approached from the vicinity of the kitchen. "Is there still time? Should we make more scallops?"

"Oh." Torn between Fred, and making an executive decision about whether to close the kitchen or not, and the mysterious man with gray eyes who obviously wanted to talk, she looked back and forth between the two.

"I see now isn't the best time to speak with you," Mr. Black spoke first. "Perhaps we can make an appointment for lunch tomorrow?"

Now she was more curious why he was at the affair. "Is there a reason to make an appointment?"

"Well, yes. A good one." He gave a confident smile. "I'm here from San Francisco, to offer you a job."

Chapter Eleven

Shortly after ten, Shelby rushed home exhilarated by success. *Titanic* night had been huge, and people were already signing on for the July Night in Paris event. Torn between the high from the successful event and shaken from the inner turmoil caused by the last-minute job offer, she needed time to think. Hadn't this been her goal when she'd come home—to find her bearings and move on? But now that she and Conor were involved again, she'd started thinking of ways to stay and be happy with the job.

She'd been approached by a total stranger who wanted to offer her a job! She'd taken a regular hotel restaurant and come up with a way to put it on the map of Central Coast, California. Both were big.

Her heart beat a happy rhythm as she took the front porch steps and hurried toward the door. If enough people showed interest, they *would* have to close the restaurant to the public to accommodate them. Who'd have ever thought the night she'd almost burned the place down that this would happen?

Conor must have heard her pull up because he opened it before she could get her key out of her purse. She threw herself into her hero's embrace. Hadn't he saved the night?

She wrapped her arms around him, careful not to spill the take-out box with several of the appetizers in it, and gave him a long, steady kiss, full of hints about what she wanted to do next. There was so much to tell him with her mind nearly exploding, and she couldn't exactly talk and kiss, so she ended it.

"You won't believe how great tonight was. I wish you could have been there." She handed him the box, and he peeked inside. "Is he asleep?"

She didn't let Conor get a word in. All he could do was nod, his eyes clearly amused by her enthusiasm. She flew to her son's door, opened it with great care, then tiptoed into the room. The sight she'd longed to see all the way home warmed her inside. If she were honest about what she'd craved, the payoff of seeing fever-free Benjamin sleeping would be a tie with seeing Conor.

Her son lay curled inward with his butt in the air, sucking his thumb. A vision only a mother would swoon over. He was so beautiful. What good fortune she had to be his mom!

Conor quietly stepped behind her, dropping his arms around her shoulders and chest and drawing her close to him. A perfect moment—being held by the man she loved and watching her son sleep. They remained that way for several seconds until Benjamin inhaled and turned away from the single bar of hallway light streaming through the door.

Once back in the living room, where Shelby's heart began calming down, her desire for Conor revved up. She zeroed in on his sensual lips and kissed him, making sure he knew exactly what was on her mind. "Surprisingly I've got a lot of energy left," she said, flicking her gaze sideways then upward to see if he read her bold message.

His arms encircled her and he took control of the next several kisses, walking her backward to her bedroom, pushing through the door and plowing onto her bed. The headboard knocked against the wall when they landed. In a matter of seconds, they'd disposed of their clothes, his hands and lips wandering to every single one of her most sensitive places. There and there, she gasped, and oh, yes, yes, there.

She lived for his sweet-tasting kisses, his heated touch. His magical fingers releasing tingles and chills over every centimeter of her body. She could let go and give in to him now, and she did for a long luxuriating while, but then she rolled him onto his back. Straddling his hips without the least bit of resistance, she had every intention of taking charge from here on out. His hooded gaze met her decided stare and he let her. Then sliding along the firm muscles of his chest and smooth stomach, inhaling his wild and turned-on scent all the way down, she descended and palmed the strong length of him, delivering a different kind of deep kiss.

Owning him.

Shelby and Conor came barreling out of her bedroom, still tucking, buttoning and zipping their clothes. She'd heard her mother's car pull into the carport a little before eleven. Feeling like a teenager all over again, she straightened her hair and hoped they didn't reek of sex.

Conor opened the box of appetizers and shoved one into his mouth before Mom came through the side kitchen door.

"How'd it go?" Donna Brookes asked, probably pretending not to notice the disheveled state of the two of them.

"Fantastic!" Shelby said, beaming. She took the box from Conor and offered her mother an appetizer. "I recommend the lamb à la française."

"Hmm, this is delicious. I'm so happy. Wish I could have been there."

"Come for the July Night in Paris event, then."

"Sign me up." Her mother distracted herself from noticing the obvious state of affairs, their disheveled appearance, by opening a catchall drawer in the kitchen, riffling through it looking for who knew what, then closing it without success.

"Mark took pictures of some of the ladies from the Prescott B&B who came in Edwardian dress, like they probably wore on the *Titanic*, and posted them on The Drumcliffe website. You would've loved them. Oh, and we had a full house, and everyone was smiling and eating like pigs. It was great."

"Wonderful. Full house?" Her mother couldn't quite bring herself to look her in the eyes, maybe because Shelby had just realized her top was buttoned all wrong, with two extras hanging noticeably over her work pants, and her lips felt swollen from their extraordinary kissing session.

Conor stood off to the side, taking everything in, having opened the container of scallop sabayon and helping himself.

"Yes. Every person who signed up showed up." Then she remembered the biggest news of the night, which, in her excitement at being with her hero and seeing her boy, had slipped her mind once home. "Oh, and you won't believe this, just as we were finishing up, some man came up to me and offered me a job in San Francisco!"

Conor went still, and so did Shelby, realizing she'd meant to tell him first, after they'd finished making love, which had gotten aborted due to her mother coming home.

"Really?" Donna seemed shocked.

"What?" Conor said, sounding unpleasantly surprised, or irritated?

"Uh, yeah, I got offered a job, but I don't know anything about it yet, because it was busy and I'm meeting this man named Damian Black for lunch tomorrow to find out more." Her face went warm.

Conor set the box on the kitchen table, tipped his head at her mother, then tossed a questioning look in her direction. "Well, when you find out the details, be sure to let me know." Sounding sarcastic and nothing like the hero whom she'd just blown the mind of. He shifted his gaze back to her mother. "Donna, now that you're home, I'll be saying good-night." He glanced back at Shelby. "I'm glad Benjamin's feeling better, and I'll talk to you tomorrow, then." And he was gone.

She couldn't let this be the way they ended their night, so she followed him out to his car. "Please don't leave like this."

"How else should I leave? You could have at least warned me that you were already looking for another job, before…" He stopped himself.

"Before what?" She hoped he'd say *before I fell in love with you again.* But that was her fantasy, and her news was clearly disturbing to him, and she'd killed their moment by blurting it out.

"Before I got attached to Benjamin."

His reply made her pause. "I'm not going anywhere.

It's just an offer." Damn, she sounded defensive. "I don't know anything yet."

"Yet." Sarcastic. He opened his car door and slid behind the wheel.

With all the hoopla of the night, she hadn't given a thought to the repercussions of Mr. Black's job offer. Only that he had. Or how the news would come off to Conor. Using the full power of his muscle car, he sped off. Good grief, how had she not thought of him?

Shaken, swinging to the dark side of the pendulum, she limped back to her house, the weight of a dozen bricks on her shoulders and with her stomach sour and twisting.

The next afternoon, Conor dressed for his evening shift, fatigued from lack of sleep. He'd had a night filled with tossing and turning and crazy dreams, one so vivid he remembered every part.

Conor cuddled Shelby closer. She'd twitched in her sleep, so he gathered her near, spooned with her, aching over losing her again. How many more times would he have to say goodbye?

Then it was back to that July six years ago.

They'd spent the best summer of their lives together in Sandpiper Beach. He'd dropped his guard, let the full force of her invade him, helpless against her. And oh, what a sweet summer it had been. Then she'd gotten the call from New York. A job she'd forgotten applying for had come through. It hadn't taken five seconds for her to make the decision. "I'll be there!" she'd said, without needing to consult anyone. Him.

Rattled, his heart shredding, he'd played it cool. "How great is that?" But in his dream he was overdoing it, laughing and pretending it was the greatest news he'd ever heard.

He'd never hold her back, turn her into the unfulfilled person his own mother had become. He'd heard the truth that day with the conversation between his grandfather and mother. "You can't have everything you want," Grandda had warned.

"It's one weekend. A chance to show my work, that's all." Mom had defended her desire to leave three little boys home with their dad and grandda for two days to share her beautiful paintings with potential buyers.

"We have a hotel to run." Padraig took the pragmatic approach, showing no mercy for his daughter-in-law, his father nowhere in sight. In the dream he looked nearly demonic, not at all like the fanciful old man talking about selkies that he was these days.

In the next part of the dream, his mother became withdrawn and quiet. He loved her and it hurt to see the sadness. Was he the only one to notice? Even at eight or nine he could tell when someone's wish had been stepped on.

Then, as dreams do, it flipped back to Shelby.

"Do you want me to go?" She asked, seeming both worried and hurt.

"You have to. It's what you want. Go for it." Again, he seemed clownish, overdoing the enthusiasm.

He'd never be the one to hold her back. Even if it meant breaking his heart.

As they walked at sunset and approached the second lifeguard station on Sandpiper Beach, he had the world's greatest idea, one that would solve all of life's problems. "Let's make a promise."

After the most complicated and disjointed dream he'd ever had, he woke up, his head aching and foggy, except for one clear thought.

Shelby had broken their promise. Now she'd probably be leaving Sandpiper Beach, too.

Hadn't he sworn he'd never let this happen again? He knew the rule book backward and forward on this. She pursues her dream, he encourages her, she leaves town, they promise to stay in touch, *they don't*, he loses her. And once more, he was going to let it happen because he never wanted to hold her back. What a fool.

Shelby had tricked him, wearing the Claddagh ring and with all her pushing for them to start over again. Why did he fall for it? Because he never wanted to do to Shelby what his dad had done to his mom. Even though his father wasn't anywhere around in that dream.

Then something Mark said when Conor had brought up the subject of his mother feeling held back by Dad and the three boys, came to mind. *Why does Mom always look so happy, then?*

Yeah, how had she gotten past her resentment and restlessness, giving up her dreams for him and his brothers?

Before he let Shelby slide another blade into his heart, he needed to have a conversation with his mom. He tucked in his undershirt and reached for his belt, then headed out the door.

"Thought I might find you here," Conor said, approaching his mother's favorite spot to paint. Instead of facing the ocean, this time she faced the hills.

"Good old predictable me," she said, flashing a self-deprecating look, then quickly got back to scattering morning glow over the brown hills.

He'd come with a purpose and decided to get right to it. "You ever wish things could've been different with your painting?"

She stopped and tossed him a curious gaze. "I get to paint every day now, what more could I want?"

"Did you ever wish you could've had a career painting?"

"With three boys, a husband and a hotel? Not likely."

He stepped closer, worried about asking the next question, but needing to for his sake, to finally know the answer. "Did you ever resent us because of that?"

She put down her palette. "What are you talking about?"

He sat on a large rock near her chair. "I have a memory of you being upset because you couldn't go to a showing or something."

"When?"

"I think I was eight or nine."

Her hands came together, her fingertips touching her lips as she thought. "Twenty or twenty-one years ago. Hmm. Oh, yes. I'd been invited to an exhibit in San Diego. I would've been gone a weekend, a very busy hotel weekend, as it turned out. Padraig and Dad needed my help." She glanced over at Conor. "I admit I was upset, but it wasn't the end of the world, and I got over it."

"I've always thought you seemed restless, Mom. Like there were other places you wanted to be. I thought maybe you resented Dad and us boys—"

"If I ever made you feel that way, Conor, I'm so sorry. Sometimes I wanted to be selfish and have time all to myself, but I've never been unhappy." She stood, came to him, put her hand on his shoulder. "Your father gave me the best gifts I could ever hope for—love, a good marriage, a home, three beautiful sons. I'd never resent that."

"But you had to put your painting on hold."

"Says who?" She planted a fist on her hip. "In case you haven't noticed, I've done a lot of oil paintings over the years, and I've also gotten better and better."

"Maybe you could've had a career."

"Never wanted one. The competition would've been unbelievable. Do you have any idea how many artists actually make a living at it?"

"So I was wrong?"

"Honey," she said, rubbing his shoulder firmly enough to jostle him around. "If you picked up on any vibes from me, it was stress from living the good life in Sandpiper Beach. The hotel could be a bear, plus the three of you kids were a handful, and with all those extracurricular activities, well, it used to make my brain spin." She shielded her eyes with her hand and stared at the ocean. "But I always had your father. We've been a good team, and he's always believed in me, and he was the one to tell me to put a painting in every single room in this old hotel."

Conor stood and hugged her, new thoughts and possibilities forming in his mind. "I guess what I was picking up was wrong, then."

"Is this about Shelby?" Mom was always good at reading his mind.

"Yes." No sense in denying it.

"She's got to figure things out all by herself."

"You're probably right."

She pulled out from the hug. "Mothers always are." Then she patted his back and he gave an ironic laugh before he headed back to his room.

"Menopause," she called out after he was a few steps away. "If you're thinking about a few years back, that is. Honey, there's just no explaining it, but I got through it." She gestured toward the ocean. "How could anyone be unhappy living with this view every single day?"

With a relieved smile over his mother's state of mind, Conor waved and let her get back to painting those craggy hills, but in typical Maureen Delaney fashion by shining shimmery golden light all over them.

* * *

Just after lunch, Conor needed to get ready for work. He slid into his uniform pants and put on some socks, then heard a knocking at his door. Opening it without a second thought, he was confronted by Shelby dressed in full interview wear, cream-colored shell top with a navy oversweater tied around her torso, and a matching navy straight skirt. He stared. Worry contorted her eyes and pursed her mouth.

"Please understand," Shelby said, willing to beg if necessary.

His brows shot up. "You took it?" His disbelief couldn't be hidden.

"No." She wanted to get that straight right off, coming inside, invited or not. "Though it is a dream job. May I sit down?"

He gestured toward a chair, then took his ironed uniform shirt off the back of another chair and slid his arms into it, giving a big hint. He had to be at work soon, so she needed to talk fast. Yet there was so much to say.

"He's a restaurant scout and he offered me an interview in San Francisco. I think, if I take the job, he gets a finder's fee or something. Anyway, it's only as sous-chef, but under a Cordon Bleu–trained chef in a posh new restaurant aiming for a Michelin star." This was the hard part, and under the time constraint she wasn't sure she could make her point without upsetting him. By the expression on his face, she already had, but she prayed he'd understand her logic. "The opportunity to learn under such a chef is astounding. I couldn't very well refuse an interview, could I? A Michelin star on my résumé could make my career!" She could come back to The Drumcliffe with her head held high, and a shiny reputation.

He searched for and chewed an antacid from his pants

pocket. God, she was making him sick. "Then why do you look so unhappy?"

Because she needed someone to bounce her thoughts off, he was her guy, he'd always been her guy. Always. Overcome with emotion, she fought for composure. He sat, quit buttoning his shirt, giving his full attention.

He had to go to work, but she needed him to understand the history, her unexplainable drive, where it came from.

"Back in New York, I sometimes felt like I was drowning in the middle of that sea of people, and no one cared. Back then, the focus of my life was all about the next great appetizer, or discovering my own special twist on any of the tried-and-true dishes. But how was I supposed to reinvent perfect?" She wound and unwound her hands, pushing her brows hard together. "If I get the job, Benjamin will need to be cared for, and my mother can't very well pick up and move with me. Plus the cost of housing there. And how do I know it won't be just like New York?" She rubbed the pinched area between her brows with her fingers. "I don't even have the job and I'm already questioning everything."

"Maybe because you already know where you and Benjamin belong."

That didn't help! She felt guilty enough. All Damian had to do was dangle a job offer in front of her, and her old yearnings came back full force. Ten years she'd waited for an opportunity like this. It'd never come in New York. Now she had a chance in another culinary mega center, San Francisco, throwing all of her sensibilities out of whack. "Do I?"

Obvious hurt briefly invaded his gaze, but before she jumped and ran to him to beg his understanding, he recovered. "Well, you won't know anything until you have that interview." So businesslike. "Do you know when it is?"

She inhaled a sudden gale of jitters. "Monday."

"I have Monday off. How about I drive to San Francisco with you? You'd probably be too nervous to take yourself, might run off the road or something."

She gave a half-hearted laugh, her lungs quivery with butterflies. "You're probably right." She latched onto his gaze, worried about how she'd come off, and grateful he hadn't thrown her out. "Would you?"

"Of course."

She stood and went to him, her anchor, invited or not, she sat on his lap and put her head on his shoulder, needing his steady peace. "It's just an interview. I swear. I need to know if all those years were wasted or not, if I finally have what it takes."

He swallowed quietly. "I'm trying to understand, but it's hard, Shel."

She wrapped her arms around his neck, squeezed tenderly. The man was a saint, and a hero, and she'd be crazy to leave him again. "What would I do without you?"

"That's something you're going to have to figure out for yourself." He gave her a chaste kiss, then broke the news to her. "I've got to leave for work."

She'd been so wrapped up in her thoughts and worries she'd been completely selfish. What did the man even see in her anyway? "Oh, right. Sorry. I'm so self-centered." She hopped off his lap, trying to make up for it with a lame compliment. "You always look handsome in your uniform."

He forced a noble smile. They walked together in silence to his car, he got inside; she needed him to understand, so she gestured for him to lower the window.

"It's just an interview."

"Yup."

"Come by for dinner tonight. I'm making salmon like you've never tasted it before."

"You bet."

She didn't believe him, the hurt in his eyes told the truth.

He backed out and drove off as she watched. Her heart should have been soaring with excitement over the interview, but it was only sore. Was reaching for that star worth losing him over?

Conor drove like a robot, he had no intention of seeing her again today. It'd hurt too damn much. He'd only last week admitted to himself that he loved her again. She'd been pushing, and he'd been the one resisting. He should have kept it up. After last night, he'd started thinking like a dad toward Benjamin, too. Hell, he'd even decided to finally put an offer on that house. So why be a fool and let her keep chasing her dreams?

Because he was the baby of the family and he'd always felt closest to his mother, and he'd always worried she wasn't happy. That he and his brothers weren't enough. Today he'd found out it wasn't them. She'd as much as sworn she'd been happy, and all that time he'd thought otherwise.

Still, there was no way he'd ever want to make Shelby unhappy. Because staying here in Sandpiper Beach, with him, had to be something she decided on her own, or he'd always have doubt. As hard as it was, he'd had no choice but to encourage her to take the interview, and risk losing her forever, because he'd never let her back in his life if she left this time.

Shelby tried her best to dive into work, explaining the night's menu to the crew and how to make it. Every moment that wasn't occupied, her mind jumped right back to Conor. Not the man she loved, but the guarded and careful guy she'd seen that afternoon. She'd done it to him again.

And he was too willing to let her go, again. History repeating itself. Maybe because San Francisco wasn't on the opposite side of the country? Still, long-distance relationships were poor excuses for couples, and they'd already tried that before. A shiver went through her. *Remember how that had turned out?*

She measured and poured soy sauce, balsamic vinaigrette, peanut and sesame oil into a large stainless-steel bowl, then added brown sugar and stirred to dissolve and blend it. Next came the diced green onions, minced garlic, salt and red pepper flakes for the salmon glaze.

When she was honest she admitted she'd always wished Conor would fight for her instead of insisting she follow her dreams. No man had ever fought for her. Her father had left and given full custody to her mother when he remarried. Over the years he'd hardly pursued a relationship with her. Laurent certainly hadn't given a damn about her, even when she'd told him they'd had a son.

Her eyes welled up, and she blamed it on too much red pepper flakes in the glaze, adding more of everything else to compensate. Still upset, she went for the freshly delivered salmon in the refrigerator, grabbed one and threw it on the cutting table. She removed the head and tail, sliced down the spine, dividing it in half, and deboned it, then made seven cuts and divided that into fourteen similar-sized pieces. One down and a dozen more to go.

Yet she was still upset. Because the only person to never break her heart had been Conor…because she broke his first. Now, instead of begging her to stay, he seemed fine with helping her get that job in San Francisco. He'd even offered to drive her there!

It's just an interview. I owe it to myself to go and see. If I don't, my time in New York will all be a waste. Ten years! She'd sacrificed so much for her dreams—how could she not go? And he'd understood too easily.

She grabbed another salmon and went to work, taking out her frustrations on the huge and gorgeous fish.

Conor had said last night he'd gotten attached to Benjamin, and that selfie with her kid proved it. But he'd yet to tell her he loved her again.

Chapter Twelve

Monday morning, Shelby's outfit was understated but chic. Or Conor could only assume, because really, what did he know about fashion? A shimmery long-sleeved loose-necked top that was almost gold and fell naturally off one shoulder, and revealing matching camisole straps beneath, fit great. Even from the parked car he could see how it picked up her huge gold-looped earrings. She wore a black pencil skirt that made him perk up when she walked down the front porch steps. He was such a sucker for her. Once she was in the car he saw how the top made her brown eyes more golden. Such beautiful eyes, why couldn't they see what was right in front of them?

Then he noticed the Claddagh ring. Right hand. Crown pointing away from her. A sign of willingness toward love. Why the hell had she worn that? To torment him even more, or was she sending a message? Damn, the woman confused him, so he insisted on ignoring the ring.

He'd been reticent yesterday, so he expected Shelby to keep trying to make him understand her side of the story this morning. Instead, she spent her time going through note cards that, he assumed, held her best recipes and also, probably, her take on the classics. He understood she needed to be prepared. At this rate, the nearly-three-hour drive to San Francisco from Sandpiper Beach would be surprisingly quiet.

Her résumé was tucked inside a folder. He knew that because she'd asked him to look it over while she bought their coffee before they finally hit the road. Her accomplishments looked great on paper. Now all she had to do was believe in herself.

He believed in her chef abilities, but couldn't understand her mercurial heart, pushing him to get back together as a couple one minute, then potentially packing up and moving away the next.

For a while she put her head back and snoozed, which made him wonder if she'd had as much trouble sleeping last night as he had. The early morning Pacific Ocean view along Highway 1 helped calm his nerves, but once they headed inland, his mind started to wander again. What could he do to get her to understand where she belonged?

She's got to figure that out herself. He hated the freaking voice of reason. Even if his mother had echoed those very words yesterday.

He gripped the steering wheel tighter, clenched his jaw and kept driving. Would she get all stressed out and forget to feed herself again if she got this job? And what about Benjamin, how would she work out his childcare? His gut twisted and it wasn't because of the extra-strong coffee he'd just downed. Shelby was responsible for that.

An hour later she woke up with a start and a quick inhale. Were her dreams as bad as his had been lately?

"Oh, my God, why'd you let me sleep? I've got to get prepared. How close are we to San Francisco?"

"Should be there in another forty-five minutes to an hour. The GPS says it'll be another twenty minutes after that to reach the restaurant."

She went silent and, instead of going over her notes again, watched out the window as small communities whizzed by and they neared their destination, passing Sunnyvale and later Redwood City.

"You know what I don't get?" He broke the silence. "Why you want this job, which is clearly a step down, now that you've been running your own first-rate kitchen? Why go back to being a sous-chef?"

"It's just an interview. To see if they'd choose me to work with a Cordon Bleu–trained chef and to help her get a Michelin star."

"Why help her? Why not earn your own Michelin star at The Drumcliffe? I think you could do it. I *know* you could."

She tossed him an incredulous look. "Do you have any idea what that would entail?"

"Enlighten me."

She folded her arms. "First off, you have to be in an area where Michelin scouts travel to even get noticed. I can assure you Sandpiper Beach isn't one of those areas."

"But you were noticed by a food scout to get this interview."

"True, but…"

"You're on the radar. Why not stay where you are and make sure you keep getting noticed? You're good enough to do that."

"I worked for ten years to get noticed. Never did. I need to see if they'd hire me."

"Why not stay where you are, help Mark turn our place

into the best restaurant it can be? You could earn a Michelin star, even though it might take ten more years, what's wrong with hard work and waiting?"

"You don't understand."

No he didn't. She was only twenty-nine, she had her whole life ahead of her. Why aim for a big award that she might never get and, in the process, lose the people who love her and the community that was already coming out to support her? He shook his head and focused back on the last part of their trip. *Open your eyes, Shelby.*

She sighed, sounding frustrated with him, then got lost in her notes again. Ahead was the Golden Gate Bridge, and she stopped reading long enough to silently look up at the beautiful sight.

He swore he wouldn't set himself up to let Shelby rip out his heart again, yet here he was driving her to the job interview that could change her life...and his. Well, it was time to spell it out, he'd been a coward keeping it to himself until now. "I love you. Can't you see that? I'm sacrificing what I want for us, for what you seem to *need* for you."

Her eyes blinked, she twisted the Claddagh ring around and around, but she didn't utter a sound. Then, after a few more seconds of silence, "I wish you would've told me that sooner."

"Would it have mattered?" Frustrated beyond belief, he'd just told her he loved her and it wasn't soon enough! He glared at the road. Besides, with her so hell-bent on making a name for herself, he doubted it would've made any difference. But he couldn't keep his mouth shut. "You think I've pushed you away every time I've encouraged you. Well, I've always felt you never bothered to consider for one second how I might feel whenever you left."

She grabbed her head. "I've got the interview of my life coming up. This is a horrible time for this conversation."

"When will it ever be the right time, Shel?" He tried to make eye contact as he said it, but she'd clearly shut down, staring at the floorboard, her lips turned in a straight line.

A few minutes later they arrived at the restaurant, Conor scoped out a place to park underground, and noticed an old coffee shop catty-corner to her appointment. He pulled to the loading zone in front of the building and let her out.

"Hey, good luck," he said as Shelby gathered her things to get out of the car.

"Thanks." She didn't look at him.

She was nervous all right—it took her two tries to open the door. When she stood, half of her note cards scattered to the ground, and she scrambled to pick them up, no easy feat in a pencil skirt.

"I'll wait across the street at that diner." He pointed.

She nodded, turned and, chin up, headed inside the building.

He didn't have a clue how long an interview for a sous-chef job would take, so he took his time parking and walked down the street. It was slow in the run-down diner, and he was able to get a window seat to keep watch. He ordered some eggs, over easy, and toast. Because his stomach was a mess with acid and knots, he skipped the coffee, but kept his eye on the building across the street.

Shelby headed straight to the ladies' room after Conor had dropped her off. She needed to clear her head, but her mind had been spinning out of control since he'd finally told her again that he loved her. What crappy timing! How could she pull her thoughts together before the interview of a lifetime?

She stared into the mirror, fixed her bangs and applied more lipstick, then gave herself a tepid pep talk. *You have to go through with this. Now is the moment of truth. You either have what it takes, or you don't. It's time to finally find out.* She pushed the elevator button for the eleventh floor, as per the instructions she'd been given. It was old and slow, and luckily, she was all by herself.

Conor had said he loved her, but he'd probably be glad to get rid of her now. Who was she kidding. History proved he wasn't like that. It'd taken a fight and a challenge for him to finally admit he loved her again, though. Could she blame him after what she'd done to him? But the best guy she'd ever met in her entire life had just said he loved her. It'd knocked the wind out of her, too. And that was what she needed, because now she finally got it. *Finally.* All those little games about a do-over and starting fresh were a bunch of lies. Of course he'd hesitate. She'd said she was ready to be with him again, but he didn't believe her because of her track record, and he was also wiser than her and saw what she couldn't. The man understood what she'd been trying to ignore. Deep down she'd still been holding out for her big break, and he knew her secret— she was still chasing her dream. How could he ever trust her when she was so out of touch with herself?

She'd always used the excuse of Conor pushing her out the door, but it'd been her who'd kept their relationship hanging all along, no matter what the collateral damage was for him, and she was still doing it.

Well, her father may have pushed her away, and Laurent, too, but Conor, the best man she'd ever known, and loved, *wasn't like them.* They'd done it for selfish reasons, but all Conor wanted was for her to be happy. Even if it meant she hurt him.

My God, how did I not figure this out?!

The elevator doors opened, and she shook her head, hoping to refocus so she could be coherent for the inter-

view. Trembling inside for a million reasons, and only a
tiny percentage over the job interview, she walked down
a deep-red carpeted hall to an office at the end, opened
the stately dark wood door and approached the stylish and
young receptionist.

"May I help you?" Way too perky for the mood Shelby
had landed in.

"Yes, I'm Shelby Brookes. Damian Black arranged an
interview for me today."

After an hour of pushing cold eggs around a plate and
pretending to read the newspaper, Conor got tired. He paid
for his meal, leaving extra for a good tip, and wandered
outside. He didn't want to go far in case Shelby came out,
so he walked a half block one way then back on one side
of the street, crossed on the light and did the same on the
other side of the street.

It wasn't the best part of town, that was for sure, and
he wanted to be right there when Shelby left, so he headed
back that way. Halfway down the block he saw her hit the
street, like she was going to the diner, and picked up his
pace to head her off.

He saw a rough-looking guy with long dirty-blond hair
pulled back in a low ponytail emerge from a doorway, look
both ways, then follow her a few steps. Worry flashed
through Conor. He couldn't lose her.

Ready to grab the guy if he tried anything, and thinking like a deputy, he took off in a sprint. The man said
something to her. She reached in her purse. No! He'd be
too late. Obviously the man planned to steal her purse,
even if it meant hurting her, then run. But before Conor
could catch up, the would-be "mugger" accepted a bill
from Shelby and turned down the next street.

Freaking out over a panhandler proved exactly how

much Conor needed Shelby, now he knew he had to stop her from making this huge mistake. *Don't leave me again.*

After Conor grabbed Shelby and held her as if for dear life, and she'd explained the situation, they'd laughed about his rushing in to save her.

"I've always dreamed about getting saved by the man I love," she said.

He kissed her like he never wanted to let her go, and she believed him.

And because they were in the beautiful city of San Francisco, the city of love, they decided to rent a room and spend the night rather than make the long drive home.

She'd just gotten off the phone with her mother, explaining the last-minute change in plans. Laurel Prescott had volunteered to watch Benjamin that morning, and promised to keep him until her mother got off work. She knew he'd been in good hands all day.

Seeing Conor running toward her, the fear on his face over a homeless man daring to ask her for change, had driven home how true and noble and downright heroic the man was. And how much he loved her. He was even willing to fight for her!

He'd finally said the words *I love you* on the drive in, too. But actions were better than words. Now there was no doubt.

Did she need a bolt of lightning to get it? He was a man worth loving, which she definitely did, and he deserved the woman he loved to stick around. Good thing she'd already come to her senses.

They checked into a hotel that cost a week's salary for one night, but figured that under the circumstances, they deserved the luxury. After taking a long sexy shower together, they pulled down the extra puffy covers on the bed.

By the time she lay back and put her head on the pillow, Conor was there, smiling over her, a look that could only be described as love in his eyes. "I thought I might have lost you today," he whispered.

She chuckled again. "You mean from the poor guy asking for coffee money?"

He moved in and they kissed in a way only two people needing to get lost in each other would.

After they'd had sex full of calisthenics and crazy positions, they ordered room service and chowed down on overpriced, mediocre hotel food. Then they made love again, this time slow and tender, so so tender. Shelby hoped Conor could read her body language and know how much she loved him. They joined together and the man never ceased to blow her mind.

Finally sated from all the goodness she could stand for one afternoon and evening, she snuggled into Conor's arms, knowing it was time to tell him what she'd learned that day.

"I noticed you haven't asked about the job."

"Did you get it?" His voice was filled with hesitation. She rushed to put her thoughts in order.

"That's a long story."

"And I want to hear every word."

"Well, first you're going to have to hear a lot of other stuff. Things I finally learned today."

"Such as?"

"Well, for instance, I know without a single doubt that a great guy named Conor lives in Sandpiper Beach, and Benjamin's grandmother, who loves to spoil him, lives there, too. I have the run of the kitchen at The Drumcliffe, and the whole Delaney clan wants to see me succeed." She turned to him and grabbed hold of his mellow gaze. "Especially my hero. You." The corner of his mouth twitched. He must've liked where she was going with this.

"That's a lot to figure out during a job interview."

Her mouth curved up, tolerating his bad attempt at a joke. "I figured out most of it on the ride in, and the rest in the elevator."

He played with the hair at her neck. "Anything else you learn?"

"Sandpiper Beach is where I grew up, and no matter how far I travel, it will always be the home of my dreams…as long as you're there."

Obviously liking all the things she'd figured out that day, he took her in his arms and kissed her long and sweetly.

How could a day that was meant to drive another wedge in their relationship wind up being perfect? Now it was her turn to kiss the hell out of him. "Thank you for not giving up on me," she said, once done.

"It wasn't a choice." His fingers caressed her cheek and jaw as a question formed in those beautiful sunny-morning, blue irises. "So? Did you get the job?"

"Yes." She gave him a second for the answer to sink in, watched the light dim in his stare and couldn't take it another cruel second. "And I turned it down. Because I love you and I want to stay with you. That is, if you still love me after how awful I've been."

"I still love you. Never stopped, just didn't want to admit it." He started to say more, but she put her finger over his lips.

"And also, it depends on if you can accept Benjamin, like a dad would, since he's never had one."

A relaxed smile stretched his mouth. "That's easy, because I already have. I've just been waiting for the word, and now that you're sticking around, I plan to put a down payment on the Beacham House. Will you and Benjamin live there with me?"

Could the guy be any more of a dream? "Yes, of course, but isn't it totally run-down?" she said as she crawled onto his body, remembering how they used to set up camp on the first floor in front of a stone fireplace where a den was supposed to be.

"Nothing a huge renovation can't fix."

As a person who'd just had a complete renovation of her attitude—love was more important than success—she knew nothing was impossible. "I believe you."

Then she used her body to show Conor how happy she was to finally see that dreams really could come true.

Chapter Thirteen

Tuesday midmorning, after the early drive home from San Francisco, Conor took Shelby to Laurel's B&B to pick up Benjamin. He'd been left there by Donna on her way to school. Benjamin squealed with happiness to see his mommy again, and something indescribable took place in Conor's heart. Feelings of honest-to-God love for the kid. Shelby had been such a huge part of Conor's life for so many years that it only seemed natural to love her son, too.

"Are you ready to see the Beacham House?" he asked finally doing the complicated job of hooking up Benny's car seat on his own.

"I'm actually nervous," she said, watching over his shoulder.

"Worried you might hate it?"

"Well, yeah, but I remember it as being a dream house, the bones of a dream house anyway." He stood and she looked straight into Conor's memories of the times they'd made love that summer. He sensed it in her moony gaze as she connected with his eyes. The upward tug at the corner of her mouth was her tell.

"That's right. Look at it that way. The shell is all there—the floors, the walls, even parts of the upstairs are almost complete." Someone, a long time ago, had started to build their dream home and something had stopped them. Some rooms were finished, others left undone. A person might think of that as bad luck, or a hex on the house, but not Conor. For him, it was all opportunity. His. "It gives us the chance to upgrade and update, and make sure that house lasts a lifetime." He wondered if she noticed his slipup saying "us" and especially "lifetime."

Her cheeks pinkened, and her nostrils flared for an instant. "Why, Conor Delaney, you sound like someone who's ready to propose."

If they were playing a staring contest, he would've won, but he had no intention of sharing every single one of his thoughts just yet. He might have plans of such things, but in his own way, and time.

She slipped silently into the car and he closed the door, then walked in front of it, knocking on the hood twice for some dumb kind of dramatic effect, got in on the driver's side, gave Shelby a deep—what he wanted to think was also mysterious—smile, then started the car and put it in gear.

A short drive into the hills later, they were on a road that cut off by itself and landed on an unremarkable bluff with a distant view of the ocean. If the Beacham House had been built somewhere else, it would've been worth millions, but having been built here, left only half-done and in disrepair for so long, no one saw its worth. Except Conor.

Sandpiper Beach wasn't a trendy enough place for people with money to want to settle in. It was a middle-class town with good enough places of business and schools. Nothing shouted, "Look at us," here. They didn't have the magnificent oceanfront that cities up the coast did, or the convenience of big city malls and Starbucks on every corner as their neighbors did to the south. Some might call the place unremarkable, but Conor preferred to judge his hometown by the number of parks and the character of the inhabitants. Starting with early settlers there like his grandfather, the community that raised Conor outside of his parents' home, and ending with the people he saw and helped every day on the job, they were what made Sandpiper Beach special. An outsider passing through wouldn't understand.

He parked, helped Shelby and Benjamin out of the car, carrying the boy himself, and led the way to the front of the house. Benny felt sturdy and warm in his arm, and he liked how the boy studied him up close before testing his morning stubble with tiny fingertips. *Yep, I'm real. And you're awfully cute.*

Some windows were installed, some weren't. There was a framed but unfinished front door that all they had to do was step around. In his mind, he saw a different kind of door with a long oval stained-glass window. He also knew the local artisan who'd been very grateful when Conor had stopped a burglary in his workshop, and who offered to give Conor a great price on stained glass any time he wanted.

He looked at Shelby and laughed. "No need for a key. Let's go in." Because he'd laughed, Benny did, too. "Yeah, let's take a look inside, huh?" And yes, he'd slipped into a goofy voice while talking to the boy. It came naturally.

Shelby was quiet, but looked everywhere. He wondered if she hated it or saw the possibilities, too.

For the next thirty minutes, they toured around the first floor, sharing their vision of what could go where. She had some great ideas, too, which relieved him. It proved she did see the house's potential.

When she started for the stairs, he stopped her. "I don't trust it's safe to go up there. Yet."

"I'd like to see the view from there."

"Follow me." He led her outside to the backyard, and pointed for her to look up. The back of the house had an upstairs deck with a huge window in what he knew was the master bedroom, giving it a lift well above the overgrown shrubs and bushes to see the ocean unhindered. "See that?"

Her eyes widened as she nodded.

"You'll be able to see the horizon on clear days, I guarantee." The hair on his arms rose as he saw his dream take hold for Shelby. Yes, she shared the dream, too.

"Look! We've already got a white picket fence." She pointed to the little run-down fence that rimmed the entire property along the back.

He loved hearing her say "we." That had been his plan all along after that amazing summer six years ago—that when they met again they'd become "we." All these years later, the Beacham House had gone into hiding thanks to natural overgrowth, and held out for him and his secret dream.

"I'm going to put a bid on the house this week."

Shelby scrunched up her shoulders and hugged herself. "How exciting."

Benny wiggled in his hold. "Yeah, one day I'll actually move out of my family's hotel."

As Conor laughed, Benny thought that was funny, too, and laughed along with him.

Conor saw it in Shelby's eyes, the waiting. She was wondering, *Will he, won't he propose?*

Shelby was the one he'd planned to ask to marry him, that night on the beach, and he couldn't forget how that had turned out. Hell, he'd even wound up tossing her engagement ring into the ocean, that was how nuts he'd gotten. The thought of asking anyone to marry him again had sent shudders through him, but she wasn't "anyone" and they'd written a few more chapters between them since she'd come home.

He took her hand, the one with the Claddagh ring, which she hadn't taken off since her interview, and began to remove it. She pulled back a bit, but gave in and let him take the lead.

"I believe it goes this way now." He took the ring from her right hand, where the crown pointed away from Shelby's heart, in the promise position, and put it on her left-hand ring finger and made sure the crown pointed toward *his* heart, to signify an engagement.

With his full attention on the person he'd loved since she'd beat him in tetherball in fourth grade, he asked, "Shelby Lyn Brookes, will you marry me?"

Moved by obvious emotion, turning deep red, she wasted no time. "You bet ya!" she said without hesitation, tears springing from her eyes as she grabbed him around the neck.

Going on tiptoe to be level with his ear, she whispered the sweetest words he'd ever heard. "Yes, yes, yes."

Epilogue

Sean and Maureen Delaney didn't waste any time renting an RV and planning a trip, the first of what they hoped would be a tradition of monthly getaways in their new semi-retirement. This one was to Cambria for a huge local artists event, then further south to Laguna Beach for the Sawdust Art Festival, to show her California Pacific Ocean series. Sean was content with being chauffeur and handling the sales aspect, since Maureen had a bad tendency to give her paintings away for a song.

All the boys had found the best women they could ever hope for, Padraig was still in excellent health and, knock on wood, so were Maureen and Sean. Now was the time to pursue their interests, alone, together. Finally.

Along with hiring two new employees, a new handyman and someone to work the front desk during the night shift, Mark and Laurel had invited Padraig to be their local ambassador for The Drumcliffe Hotel. *'Tis the best view for a wedding anywhere along the Central Coast of California*, he'd tell anyone at the drop of a hat, while handing out postcards in public venues, then often add, *except for maybe Sligo Bay back home in Ireland.*

Laurel had tapped Shelby's culinary talent for ways to upgrade the Prescott B&B's offerings. Laurel had also come up with a spectacular wedding package idea, including all catering, one that was bound to draw more interest and new customers thanks to Shelby's growing reputation as the hot new chef on the Central Coast.

Even Padraig had suggested a golf package for guests, by partnering at a discount with The Sandpiper Beach Golf club, and offering to personally shuttle those who signed up to and from the beautiful golf course in his four-seater electric golf cart. What better advertising for the eclectic older hotel than a wee touched, brightly dressed Irishman walking the streets of Sandpiper Beach using his golf club as a cane, spouting the magic of The Drumcliffe, leaving postcards for the hotel in all the local businesses?

Often enough, he was still known to stop anyone on the street or in the pub who'd listen with his favorite opening line. "Did I ever tell you about the time my grandsons saved a selkie?"

In late fall, Daniel, Mark and Conor met up for a beer at the family pub one quiet Sunday afternoon. As often was the case whenever they had the chance to get together, they talked about all the changes that had happened since their first ever fishing trip a year and a half ago, over a Guinness. The infamous day they'd saved a seal from a pod of orca.

"Do you think Grandda was right about us saving the seal?" Conor ventured to ask after a long draw on his glass.

"That we actually saved a selkie and that's why we've all found our wives?" Daniel mocked the possibility while raising the forbidden question, the one that nagged way in the back of each brother's mind, especially whenever they marveled over their good fortune since saving that seal.

Mark stayed silent, not making eye contact. Neither Conor nor Daniel said a word, either. They each thought over the meaning of what their fantastical-thinking grandfather said about debts owed and paid, and his predictions about selkies.

Could the selkie folklore possibly be true?

After a moment, each brother raised his glass at the exact same time, still hesitating to face the question. Daniel looked at Conor, then Conor looked at Mark, all with the unspoken question written in their eyes, then Mark looked at Daniel, who looked again at Conor with tension building in their silence.

True?

"Nah," they said in unison, relieved, before taking another drink, settling on coincidence for their good fortune.

Then Grandda and Brian came rushing into the pub on a wave of excitement. Grandda took off his flat cap and tossed it on the bar. "You won't believe what Brian, here, did this afternoon."

"Golf a level-par game?" Daniel piped up.

"No. I did that, son," Grandda said with his cheeky grin. "See, we were looking for his ball, in the beach sand, when down the way, we spied a seal all tangled in seaweed and the good Lord only knew what else, making a dreadful sound." Padraig looked around to make sure he had the attention of each of his grandsons. And Conor had a sinking feeling about exactly where this story was going.

"Brian, boyo, didn't take a second to think, just stepped

over and helped untangle that poor seal, and sent her on her way."

"The seal swam off okay?" Mark asked in an obvious effort to change the subject.

"Not before looking back, lad." There was that overly stretched grin again.

"Hey, Brian, good for you saving a seal," Daniel interrupted.

"Not a seal," Grandda said. "A *selkie*, and she had a smile on her face as broad as the Shannon." Kind of like the one Conor saw on his grandfather's face.

The brothers shared an indulgent laugh, mainly to humor the old man. Then Conor checked out Brian to see if he was buying any of Grandda's malarky. Didn't look like it, thank goodness, only that he was amused.

"So, Grandda," Conor spoke up when things quieted down. "Are you saying *all* seals are selkies?"

The old man made his "how absurd" face, brows crunched down, mouth screwed up. "No, lad, are ya daft?"

Then his expression went serene and there was that familiar faraway twinkle in his eyes.

"Only the ones saved by a Delaney."

*   *   *   *   *

Don't miss out on the other Delaney brothers' stories:

FOREVER A FATHER
SOLDIER, HANDYMAN, FAMILY MAN

Available now from Harlequin Special Edition!

And if you love second chance romances,
try these great books:

FROM EXES TO EXPECTING
By Laurel Greer

THE FORTUNE MOST LIKELY TO...
By Marie Ferrarella

A KISS, A DANCE & A DIAMOND
By Helen Lacey

Available wherever Harlequin Special Edition
books and ebooks are sold!

COMING NEXT MONTH FROM

HARLEQUIN®

SPECIAL EDITION

Available May 22, 2018

#2623 FORTUNE'S HOMECOMING
The Fortunes of Texas: The Rulebreakers • by Allison Leigh
Celebrity rodeo rider Grayson Fortune is seeking a reprieve from the limelight. So as his sweet real estate agent, Billie Pemberton, searches to find him the perfect home, he struggles to keep his mind on business. Grayson is sure he's not cut out for commitment, but Billie is convinced that love and family are Grayson's true birthright...

#2624 HER SEVEN-DAY FIANCÉ
Match Made in Haven • by Brenda Harlen
Confirmed bachelor Jason Channing has no intention of putting a ring on any woman's finger—until Alyssa Cabrera, his too-sexy neighbor, asks him a favor. But their engagement is just for a week...isn't it?

#2625 THE MAVERICK'S BRIDAL BARGAIN
Montana Mavericks • by Christy Jeffries
Cole Dalton thought letting Vivienne Shuster plan his wedding—to no one—would work out just fine for both of them. But now not only are they getting caught up in a lot of lies, they might just be getting caught up in each other!

#2626 COMING HOME TO CRIMSON
Crimson, Colorado • by Michelle Major
Escaping from a cheating fiancé in a "borrowed" car, Sienna Pierce can't think of anywhere to go but Crimson, the hometown she swore she'd never return to. When Sheriff Cole Bennet crosses her path, however, Crimson starts to look a little bit more like home.

#2627 MARRY ME, MAJOR
American Heroes • by Merline Lovelace
Alex needs a husband—fast! Luckily, he doesn't actually need to be around, so Air Force Major Benjamin Kincaid will do perfectly. That is, until he's injured—suddenly this marriage of convenience becomes much more than just a piece of paper...

#2628 THE BALLERINA'S SECRET
Wilde Hearts • by Teri Wilson
With her dream role in her grasp, Tessa needs to focus. But rehearsing with brooding Julian is making that very difficult. Will she be able to reveal the insecurities beneath her dancer's poise, or will her secret keep them apart?

HSECNM0518

SPECIAL EXCERPT FROM

H HARLEQUIN®

SPECIAL EDITION

*Cole Dalton thought letting Vivienne Shuster
plan his wedding—to no one—would work out just
fine for both of them. But now not only are they getting
caught up in a lot of lies, they might just be getting
caught up in each other!*

*Read on for a sneak preview of
the next **MONTANA MAVERICKS** story,
THE MAVERICK'S BRIDAL BARGAIN
by Christy Jeffries.*

"You're engaged?"

"Of course I'm not engaged." Cole visibly shuddered. "I'm not even boyfriend material, let alone husband material."

Confusion quickly replaced her anger and Vivienne could only stutter, "Wh-why?"

"I guess because I have more important things going on in my life right now than to cozy up to some female I'm not interested in and pretend like I give a damn about all this commitment crap."

"No, I mean why would you need to plan a wedding if you're not getting married?"

"You said you need to book another client." He rocked onto the heels of his boots. "Well, I'm your next client."

Vivienne shook her head as if she could jiggle all the scattered pieces of this puzzle into place. "A client who has no intention of getting married?"

"Yes. But it's not like your boss would know the difference."

"She might figure it out when no actual marriage takes place. If you're not boyfriend material, then does that mean you don't have a girlfriend? I mean, who would we say you're marrying?"

Okay, so that first question Vivienne threw in for her own clarification. Even though they hadn't exactly kissed, she needed reassurance that she wasn't lusting over some guy who was off-limits.

"Nope, no need for a girlfriend," he said, and she felt some of her apprehension drain. But then he took a couple of steps closer. "We can make something up, but why would it even need to get that far? Look, you just need to buy yourself some time to bring in more business. So you sign me up or whatever you need to do to get your boss off your back, and then after you bring in some more customers—legitimate ones—my fake fiancée will have cold feet and we'll call it off."

If her eyes squinted any more, they'd be squeezed shut. And then she'd miss his normal teasing smirk telling her that he was only kidding. But his jaw was locked into place and the set of his straight mouth looked dead serious.

Don't miss
THE MAVERICK'S BRIDAL BARGAIN
by Christy Jeffries,
available June 2018 wherever
Harlequin® Special Edition books and ebooks are sold.

www.Harlequin.com